More Adventures of
SAMURAI CAT

More Adventures of
SAMURAI CAT

Mark E. Rogers

TOR
A TOM DOHERTY ASSOCIATES BOOK

MORE ADVENTURES OF SAMURAI CAT

Copyright © 1986 by Mark Rogers
All rights reserved, including the right to reproduce this book or portions thereof in any form.

First printing: November 1986
Printed in Spain by Printer I.G.S.A.
Sant Vicenç dels Horts   Barcelona   D.L.B.: 25711-1986
A TOR Book

Published by Tom Doherty Associates
49 West 24 Street • New York, N.Y. 10010
ISBN: 0-812-55248-2   CAN. ED.: 0-812-55249-0

0 9 8 7 6 5 4 3 2 1

To my mother-in-law Bobbie Jean,
who has been a great help over the years.

Contents

I. A Samurai Cat in King Arthur's Court

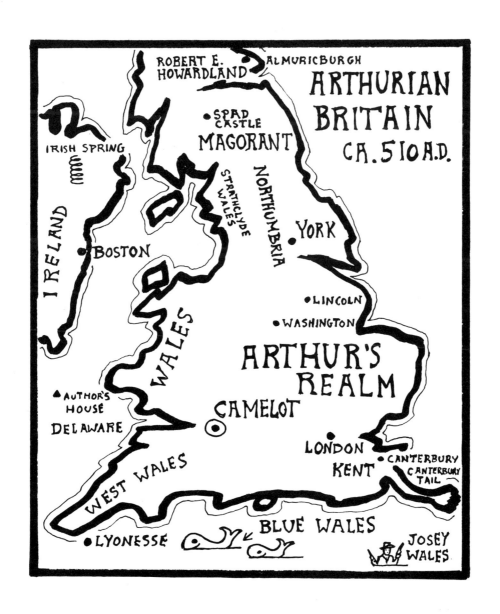

ARTHURIAN BRITAIN CA. 510 A.D.

ROBERT E. HOWARDLAND

ALMURICBURGH

SPAD CASTLE

MAGORANT

IRISH SPRING

STRATHCLYDE WALES

NORTHUMBRIA

YORK

IRELAND

BOSTON

LINCOLN

WASHINGTON

WALES

ARTHUR'S REALM

AUTHOR'S HOUSE

DELAWARE

CAMELOT

LONDON

KENT

CANTERBURY

CANTERBURY TAIL

WEST WALES

BLUE WALES

LYONESSE

JOSEY WALES

Upon leaving Asgard and seeing Shiro off, Tomokato turned his attention to the next man on his list—Mordred, a renegade British prince who had led a contingent of Saxon barbarians to the slaying of Nobunaga. Learning that his prey was studying insurgency (Terrorism 305 and Destabilization 406) at Moscow's Patrice Lumumba University, the cat went to the Soviet capital posing as a Comintern representative from sixteenth-century Japan, only to discover that Mordred had already graduated magna cum laude, and was back raising an army in Britain. Having aroused the suspicion of the authorities, Tomokato secretly hitched a ride with a Mongol horde, on their way to an assault on Indiana, and got off at Northumbria, right in the middle of Mordred's territory . . .

From: Cat Out of Hell; A Biography of Miaowara Tomokato,
by William Shirer and A.J.P. Godzilla

On a chill, leaden October day, Arthur, King of the Britons, stood with his closest knights and Merlin his counselor on the outer wall of Camelot, watching a group of armored riders approach through the drear landscape. Above the horsemen streamed a flag of truce, and a red-and-black banner showing a knife buried to the hilt in an innocent-looking back. The foremost rider had his helmet off; recognizing him, Arthur shook his head ruefully.

"I still can't believe he's my son," he muttered.

"If only it were not so, My Lord," said Merlin beside him.

"Looks more like that damn Federal Express man than me," Arthur went on.

"How many times must we go through this, My Lord?" Merlin asked wearily. "The blood test proved you were the one. Why do you think we lost on that paternity rap—"

"Greetings, Father!" called Arthur's son, halting his troop at the foot of the drawbridge.

"Won't you come inside, Mordred?" Arthur cried. "Must we shout at each other?"

"It's better than being caught in a trap," Mordred jeered.

"You know me better than that. I wouldn't break the truce. And besides, if I wanted your life, my Welsh bowmen would have shot you dead a hundred yards from these walls."

Mordred laughed. "Just being obnoxious, Father. The truth is, I wish to endure your company as briefly as possible, and then only at a distance, and downwind."

"Oh yeah?" shouted Sir Gawaine, who had heard more than enough.

Mordred curled one horn of his black moustache, laughing satanically, sable cloak billowing behind him in the wind. "Yeah," he replied.

"Enough," Arthur cried, raising a hand. "What are your terms, Mordred?"

"First, you must name me your sole heir," Mordred replied. "Secondly, you must name me coregent and acknowledge my claim to the lands I've already taken."

"Is that all?" Arthur laughed, marveling at his son's arrogance.

"No. I also want to name and preside over a new Central Economic Committee, with powers and responsibilities to be defined by me. The only way we're going to get out of this

balance-of-trade situation is with a solid dose of industrial planning, and I'm just the boy to see it through."

"Are you?" Arthur demanded. "Milton Friedman says your policies are hogwash."

"Milton Friedman?" Mordred cried. "Give me a break!"

"Why don't you give us all a break, Mordred?" Arthur pleaded. "Give up these mad schemes. Put aside your hatred. Become a monk. Go far far away. Or kill yourself, maybe."

"Soothing words," Mordred answered. "But words won't save you."

"Even if I agree to your terms?"

"No, not even then."

"God in heaven, you're irrational."

"Yeah, I know. And I just love it." With that, Mordred planted a loud, smacking kiss on his own left hand. "Be seeing you, Dad. I'll be back—with my army."

He and his company turned and galloped off.

"Merlin," Arthur said, "what are our chances?"

Merlin stroked his white beard thoughtfully.

"As things stand now, My Lord, I'd say we're up the proverbial creek."

"What's the latest word on his forces?"

"Every day another of your subject kings flocks to his banner."

"Can a single man flock?"

"Hey look, Sire, I'm a wizard, not a grammarian," Merlin snapped. "Now where was I? Oh, yes. A huge Saxon army under Horsa's son Mister Ed has crossed the channel. It'll be joining Mordred's host within the week—along with the usual compliment of East German and North Korean advisers. The Cubans have also finished that airstrip outside York. Mordred's troops are receiving more Warsaw Pact weapons than they could ever possibly use. With armor support."

"Armor?"

"Chain mail, plate, the works."

"You're sure he's getting it from the Eastern Bloc?"

"Positive, Sire." Merlin signaled a knight forward, Sir Lew De Grade; in his arms the man bore a shirt of crudely-made chain, as well as a primitive but reliable-looking mace. Arthur took the weapon, hefted it.

"An AK-1," Merlin said. "Warsaw Pact, standard issue."

"Good Lord," Arthur said. "How can we stop him?"

"We'll lay down our lives, all of us," said Sir Lancelot. "Give the last drop of our blood."

"Not me," said Sir Gareth. "I gave last week."

"We cannot win through force of arms," Merlin said.

"Shall we just despair, then?" Arthur asked. "Hope to die well, and nothing more?"

"No, there's a chance. We must trust in God. And the Prophecy."

"You mean the one about the Antichrist and the Common Market?"

"No," Merlin said solemnly. "The one about the Holy Spad."

"The Spad," Arthur said. "The plane Joseph of Arimathea flew the Holy Grail to Britain in."

Merlin nodded. "Only a Knight of the Round Table who has achieved the Spad can defeat Mordred."

"But achieving the Spad . . ." Arthur said. "No one's ever come close. Not even Jacques Cousteau . . . Of course, he kept looking for it in the South Pacific, so what do you expect?"

"You must hold a tourney, Sire," Merlin continued. "Find the strongest knight in your realm and send him on the quest."

"But will there be enough time?" Arthur asked.

"Sure. Mordred's already announced that he'll be attending a wine-tasting in some place called Chemung, New York. His troops will have to wait till he returns."

"Very well then. A tourney will be held. Make the preparations."

They went down from the parapet.

"Blood test, schmudtest," Arthur muttered. "How could I have a kid like that?"

The day of the tournament came, bright and warm despite the grim weather that had preceded it; golden light flooded the huge main courtyard of Camelot, where the jousting was to be held. At the appointed time, a trumpet summoned the knights, and to the cheers of the onlookers, they rode to the lists, a glorious company resplendent in many-colored surcoats. Most were Knights of the Round Table, but some were warriors of other realms who had proven their mettle in preliminary jousts the day before.

One of these outland knights had already created quite a stir because of his unusual and devastating technique—using a blunted two-handed sword against opponents with lances. Fully ten warriors had been unhorsed by him, including several of Arthur's less experienced retainers. This knight was small in stature and never revealed his face; no man knew his name. He spoke but little, and he had no squire. There was much speculation as to where he was from; he would say only, "From the east," and some took this to mean he was French, or German, or even a Christianized Saracen. But wherever his home, he was clearly a foe to be reckoned with, and his prospective opponents were eager to test their lances against his terrible sword.

Once the knights had assembled, the Master of the Lists bade them salute the king in his pavilion, then recited the rules of the tourney and told of the commission that would be laid upon the victor: to find the Holy Spad, bring it to Camelot, and use it to thwart Mordred's armies, the glory of this enterprise being more valuable by far than any prize.

Having spoken, the Master took up his horn once more, blew a single ringing note, then cried: "Let the first combatants enter the lists!"

Forth they rode at a walk, having been chosen by lot, the small outlander among them, ten in all; five to a side, they took their places in the lists, between the brightly-colored partitions. An expectant hush fell over the crowd.

The Master's horn sounded yet again. The knights spurred their mounts, goading them forward. Swiftly the beasts picked up speed, the thunder of their hooves echoing hollowly between the walls of the courtyard. Helms and shields flashed, lances dipped; with a titanic shock the sides clashed together. Lances thumped and clattered from bucklers, shivered into flying fragments. Bodies rocked backward over cantles, spinning head over heels.

When it was done, six men lay groaning in the dust, Sir Sagramor and Sir Freddy Laker having unhorsed each other. And the mystery knight was among the victors.

It was three more rounds before he jousted again, this time against Sir Bedivere; hacking so mightily that his blunted edge chopped Bedivere's lance into several score bite-sized chunks,

he swept the bewildered knight from his saddle with the flat of his blade, pitching him earthward to the gasps of the crowd. Two rounds later, Sir Dinadan took a similar beating, and two rounds after that, Sir Laurence Olivier was carried from the yard quoting dazedly from *Richard III*. As the field narrowed, the pattern was played out again and again, until only Gawaine and Lancelot, the mightiest of Arthur's knights, remained to defend the honor of the Round Table against the stranger.

As Gawaine charged toward the mysterious warrior, he employed a stratagem which had given him many victories in the past: keeping his lance couched well back and leaning back in his saddle, all the while restraining the speed of his mount—until the last moment, when he leaned forward, thrust out with his weapon, and dug his spurs powerfully into his horse's flanks. His lance-tip plunged close to the other knight's chest, even seemed to touch it; the onlookers roared, delighted that someone had gotten past the stranger's guard at last.

Then came the squeal of split wood, and the halves of the lance passed on either side of the stranger, parted down the middle by a single ferocious blow of that edgeless sword. As Gawaine swept by howling a Welsh victory cry—something about Roarke's Drift—his antagonist rapped him smartly across the face-plate with the flat of his blade and sent him hurtling back over his horse's rump yodeling with black Celtic despair.

Now only Lancelot Du Lac stood between the stranger and victory. The outlander was already waiting for him as he entered the lists. For a few moments the opponents eyed each other, awaiting the Master's signal; the courtyard was dead quiet save for the lazy flap of windblown pennons atop the pavilions. Then the horn-blast came, and the two warriors thundered to the onset.

The foreigner made to strike at Lancelot's lance; Lancelot swept it out of the way, thinking to bash it sideways against his foe's helm. Missing his first stroke, the stranger instantly lashed out with a second, breaking Lancelot's weapon in two. But there was still enough of a stump to bring down on the mystery knight's helmet, and the stranger was almost unhorsed then and there, wobbling in his saddle as he rode to the end of the list.

They faced each other again. The outlander straightened, apparently recovering. But Lancelot, taking a second lance from his squire, guessed his foe must be at least partially dazed by such a mighty blow, and thought Gawaine's stratagem would be a good way to finish him if carried out swiftly enough; confident of victory, he galloped forward as the Master's horn belled forth its note.

Straight toward him his opponent came, sword flashing, shearing off the first two feet of Lancelot's weapon as Lancelot launched his sudden thrust; then the jagged end was plunging straight toward the foreigner's face-plate. Lancelot laughed, sure he had him.

But that was before the mystery knight bounded high into the air, out of the saddle, and lit midway along the spear.

You gotta be kidding, was all Lancelot had time to think, watching him come running surefootedly up the shaft. Then that two-handed brand beaned him but good.

As Lancelot rocked backward from his horse, drifting blissfully into chivalrous nirvana, the outlander dropped into Lancelot's saddle, slowed the horse to a canter, then a walk, and rode over to the king's pavilion.

The spectators were going wild; as much as they hated to see the home team beaten so badly, they had never seen such feats of arms.

"What a stud," said Merlin to Arthur as the victor approached.

"Sir knight," Arthur called, "you have been victorious, and have earned the right to seek the Spad. What are you called, and what land produces such mighty warriors?"

"My name is Miaowara Tomokato," the knight replied, dismounting; with several movements almost too fast to see, he swept off his helmet and unzippered his mail, stepping out of it, revealing a full suit of laced lamellar armor underneath. "As for my country, I come from Japan."

"He's a *cat*," Merlin gasped.

"Worse than that," said Gawaine, who had drawn near with the crowd of defeated knights. "He's a *Japanese* cat!"

"Well, so what if he is Japanese?" Arthur asked.

"With all due respect, Sire," Gawaine said, "if you'll recall our agreement . . ."

"What agreement? . . ." Arthur paused. "Oh. You mean that protectionist thing?"

"Sire," said Lancelot, staggering up beside Gawaine, "if it wasn't for that 'protectionist thing,' as you call it, this court would be overrun with samurai, taking work away from us Europeans. Just think about it, My Lord. A large and growing Japanese population in the heart of Britain. What about when World War II comes along? Can we really afford to have a fifth column like that?"

"What are you talking about?" Arthur demanded. "All we have here is one Japanese cat who won the tourney fair and square. . . ."

"Sire," Gawaine began, "under our agreement, no Japanese is allowed to enter one of our tournaments, and that's final."

"Final?" Arthur cried. "How dare you tell me what's final? I'm the Once and Future King!"

"Maybe so, My Lord. But I'm president of Local 233. You want to tangle with the Teamsters?"

At the mention of the Teamsters, Arthur twitched a nervous smile, raising his hands. "Now just hold on. I'm sure we can work something out here. Just consider him a one-time exception. After all, we really need him. There's no better man—I mean *cat*—for the job."

The knights grumbled at that.

"Complain all you like," Arthur said, "but

he whaled the hell out of you."

"Think of it this way," Merlin told them. "How's your local going to fare if Mordred wins? He won't be bringing in Japanese, maybe, but what about Saxons? They work for nothing. Give 'em a hole to sleep in with a hog to keep 'em warm, and they're happy as clams."

"But he's not even a Knight of the Round Table," Lancelot said, jerking a thumb toward Tomokato. "The Prophecy says that's what it'll take."

"Your king could knight me," Tomokato said.

"But how do we know you won't grab the Spad and fly off with it?" Gawaine asked suspiciously.

"Because I want Mordred's blood as much as you do," Tomokato replied. "He was with the horde that murdered My Lord Nobunaga. I've already tried to kill him several times, but the most amazing circumstances prevented me."

"What circumstances?" Arthur asked.

"The first time, I was struck by lightning," Tomokato said. "The second time, I was struck by an elephant falling out of a clear blue sky. The third time, I was transported mysteriously to French Guiana. On the boat back to Britain, I concluded that the Fates were against me. But then I learned of the Prophecy and realized

what I had to do—become a Knight of the Round Table and achieve the Spad."

"Very well then," Arthur said. "If there are no objections . . ." He looked at Gawaine, who shrugged sourly. "You'll have your chance, Tomokato. I'll knight you here and now." He turned to several men-at-arms. "Fetch me Excalibur," he commanded.

After some time they returned, lugging a large hunk of granite with a splendid gold-hilted sword thrust into it. Arthur had made his way down from the stand; they set it in front of him, panting.

"The Sword in the Stone," Arthur told Tomokato. "When I withdrew it in my youth, I was proclaimed King."

"But why is it back in the stone?" Tomokato asked.

"Mordred smeared Crazy Glue all over it and shoved it back in the slot," Arthur answered. "Last thing he did before he left home. I can still hear him shouting as he rode off: 'You can do some *crazy* things with it!'"

"Is it true that he's your son?" Tomokato asked. "What an unnatural child!"

"Actually," Arthur said, "he's my sister's kid." Merlin coughed.

"In any case," Arthur told the cat, "let's get you knighted. Kneel, Tomokato."

Tomokato knelt. Arthur signaled to the men-at-arms, who, grunting with exertion, lifted the boulder and positioned Excalibur over the cat, Arthur taking hold of the hilt.

"I, Arthur, *Rex Brittanorum*, dub you *Sir Miaowara Tomokato*, Knight of the Round Table, in the name of God and St. George.". With that, Arthur and the soldiers lowered the blade, touching the cat on either shoulder. "Rise, Sir Tomokato."

Tomokato got to his feet. "Now, Sire," he said. "How do I find the Spad?"

Accompanied by Arthur, Merlin led Tomokato up to his tower study, there to consult his book of maps. Bound in the skin of a gryphon that had once been Merlin's pet—Merlin had called him Merv—the tome rested atop a stand crafted from unicorn horns and the finest Thracian Lucite. Merlin cracked the book open to the *M*'s and started riffling through the maps.

"Macao, Macedon, Mackinac Island . . ." he said, under his breath.

"The castle's located in the land of Magorant," said Arthur to Tomokato. "A realm from which no one's ever returned."

"Then how could you possibly have a map of it?" Tomokato asked.

"Merlin went up to the border a few years ago and yelled across—asked if he could borrow one."

"They fell for that?" Tomokato asked, incredulous.

"No, but a voice howling on the wind suggested he have a photograph of Magorant taken from a satellite."

"Ah, here we are," Merlin said, motioning them over. Place-names meticulously calligraphed in Carolingian Minuscule, the map showed a large portion of Northumbria as well as Magorant.

"How did you learn the place-names?" Tomokato asked.

"They're written on the actual landscape," Merlin said. "We theorize that a bunch of Incas came over and stenciled 'em all in a while back."

"Strange," Tomokato said.

"This island's full of strange things," Arthur said. "And it attracts strange people. Why just the other day, we put a halt to a construction project down on Salisbury Plain, called Stonehenge. Owner was passing himself off as a Druid, said he was just building an observatory. But we found out he was actually trying to create bogus evidence that the earth has been visited by extraterrestrials. Name was Von Daniken. We deported him."

"Can I take the map with me?" Tomokato asked Merlin.

"Out of the question," Merlin said. "I don't loan my maps to *anyone*."

"Could you provide me with a copy?"

"Yes, but it'll take a couple of days. Our machine's broken, and we're waiting for the repairman."

Tomokato scrutinized the map. "I don't see Spad Castle."

"There it is," Merlin said, indicating a tiny grey spot. "At least, we think that's it."

"There's no place-name," Tomokato observed.

"True. But detail analysis confirms the presence of a large number of Inca skeletons piled nearby. We think they were killed before they could do the calligraphy."

"Which is how we know it's Spad Castle," Arthur said. "The fortress is owned by Morgan Le Fairchilde, Mordred's mother—she built it to keep the Spad from people who would use it against her son. She once gave an interview in which she bragged openly about slaughtering a bunch of Third-World types who tried to letter her valley."

"Sounds like a very dangerous woman," Tomokato said.

"In any number of ways," Arthur said. "She has vast powers of magic. She can transform herself at will. One night she showed up here at Camelot disguised as the Pointer Sisters. I didn't even recognize her, and . . ." The king's voice trailed off.

"She'll try to deceive you, Tomokato," Merlin said. "She'll do anything to keep you from the Spad. When you reach the castle, you must remain constantly on guard."

"But do me one favor," Arthur said. "Don't kill her unless you have to."

"I never kill unnecessarily," Tomokato replied.

Merlin raised an eyebrow. "You don't think the slaughter in these stories *ever* gets gratuitous?" he asked.

"I didn't say that. But I always act properly, given the circumstances I find myself in." Tomokato paused. "So you think it'll be a couple of days till the repairman arrives, eh?"

Merlin nodded.

"Ah well," said the cat. "I suppose it can't be helped."

"Not if you want the map," Merlin said.

"Aching to be out on the quest?" Arthur asked Tomokato.

"I ache to fulfill my duty."

"Such rectitude," Merlin said.

"It's nothing," said the cat, with the genuine modesty of the naturally superb.

A week later, in a rugged defile where a checkpoint marked the boundary between Mordred's territory and Arthur's, Lieutenant Erich Von Stroheim, an adviser from the East German Army, was instructing the sentries in the fine art of planting controlled substances on incoming vehicles when Tomokato came riding serenely toward them, reading a paperback edition of *Zen and the Art of Motorcycle Mainte-*

nance.

"Halt!" Von Stroheim cried, raising his hand, the mailed British sentries shouldering up on either side of him. Tomokato stopped a few yards from the gate.

"What's that you're reading?" Von Stroheim asked.

"Watered-down Buddhism," Tomokato replied. "Picked it up at a truckstop—trash. Would you like it?"

Von Stroheim sneered, fingering the dueling-scar on his cheek. "Are you insulting me?"

"Certainly not."

"State your name and business."

"My name's Miaowara Tomokato," the cat answered. "I review books for a Japanese magazine called *Starlog*."

"And what is the purpose of your visit to Lord Mordred's realm?"

"I've been sent to attend an ABA convention in York."

"Aren't you taking a very roundabout route?"

"I was told this was the most scenic way to go."

"You're very heavily armored for a book reviewer," Von Stroheim observed.

"I have many enemies. I write very negative reviews."

"Really?" Von Stroheim asked. "You know what I think?"

Tomokato eyed him steadily. "No, what?"

"I think you're a spy from King Arthur."

Tomokato shook his head. "Don't you know that he doesn't employ Japanese?"

"I've seen lots of Japanese," Von Stroheim grated. "You're some kind of animal." He blew a whistle, and suddenly, flinging their hogs aside, a score of Saxons in leather scales and boar-crested helms came bursting up out of holes behind the guard-posts. Brandishing swords and spears, they raced toward the East German, who pointed to the cat.

"Take him!" Von Stroheim cried, and the sentries raised the gate to let the Saxons through.

As the foremost barbarian drew near the cat, Tomokato plucked a spiked throwing-star, or *shuriken*, from the specially constructed *shuriken* bin attached to his saddle and pegged the missile hard into the man's throat, turning a fearsome battle cry into a gurgly *UKKKKKK* in midwhoop. A second Saxon caught one in the eye, a third in the brain, clear through the front of his boar-helm. Moving almost too fast for the eye to see, and certainly too fast for even the semblance of fair play, Tomokato felled half the onrushing mob before he ran out of stars—by which point the remaining Saxons were so petrified that he had time to casually drop *Zen and the Art of Motorcycle Maintenance*, snatch up his bow, string it, and nock an arrow.

"I knew you weren't a book reviewer!" Von Stroheim cried, grabbing a spear from a Saxon, cocking it back to hurl at the cat.

"But I *am* Japanese," Tomokato replied, loosing the arrow, clearing out the East German's sinuses with a shot smack into his nose.

"*Ach Du Lieber!*" cried the Saxons as Tomokato nocked another arrow, and with the sentries, they ran off down the defile, their hogs running desperately to keep up, oinking forlornly.

Tomokato rode unhurriedly through the checkpoint.

In the days that followed, Tomokato pushed steadily northwestward into Mordred's land. For the people living under the rebel prince's harsh rule, things seemed to have deteriorated even in the few weeks since the cat had traveled through this territory. The rule of Right over Might, Arthur's proudest achievement, had totally decayed, with kings and lords who had once sworn fealty to Arthur now oppressing the population in Mordred's name, looting the towns to pay the upkeep on ever-growing armies of ruffians and bandit knights; companies of Saxons roved everywhere, holding riotous *Oktoberfests* whenever they felt like it, going on drunken rampages, plundering monasteries and killing churchmen, setting up heathen altars to Woden and Thunor and the detestable Barry Manilow. The economy was in a shambles, beggars and gas lines everywhere, and the press had been muzzled; more than once Tomokato saw rotting corpses hanging from trees, placards tied to their necks proclaiming them London *Times* reporters or correspondents from CNN.

Mordred's security forces attacked Tomokato repeatedly, but each time he escaped unscathed, leaving behind a broad wake of death and devastation, some of which (like when he cut this

one guy *and* his horse in two) was really juicy, but I don't have time to go into it here; suffice it to say, he stirred up quite a hornet's nest and was being tailed by a huge detachment of Apache trackers as he neared the border of Magorant.

Yet as he entered that grim land, a drear waste of crags and tarns and dank valleys, he realized he was no longer being followed; whether the Apaches were afraid to set foot there or merely thought he would never return or both, he had no way to tell. But as he soon discovered, Magorant more than lived up to its grim reputation.

First there were the black knights, in all shapes and sizes, contesting every bridge or pass. Then there were the water-maidens, beings fair in appearance who tried to lure him beneath the surfaces of their dark pools with promises of illicit pleasure or riches or Reese's Pieces, or the damnedest collection of videotapes in all Christendom. More terrible were the Junkies Sauvage of the Screaming Caves and the Disco Dwarves Sans Pitié of the Ragged Wood. Worst of all were the Three Lords of the IRS, against whom Tomokato's swordsmanship and knowledge of the tax codes only barely prevailed. But finally he saw before him, halfway up the slope of a jagged mountain honeycombed with red-glowing cave-mouths, the walls and towers of Spad Castle.

The fortress did not seem to fit in at all with its surroundings, with its pink stone and decorative casements; more than anything else, it reminded him of a postcard of the Magic Kingdom that Shimura had sent him from Disney World. Warily he rode up the winding, treacherous path toward the open gate. As far as he could tell, there was no one on the battlements. Coming up to the gatehouse, he rode slowly in under the portcullis, his horse's hooves clopping hollowly in the gate-tunnel. Entering the spacious courtyard, he saw it was deserted. The cobbles seemed to be wet, as if with a recent rain; then he caught a whiff of polish, and realized that they had recently been *waxed*. Brightly-colored heraldic banners hung from the surrounding walls, along with flags of the United Nations. Off to the right were a replica of Michelangelo's "David" and a statue of Cale Yarborough, defiantly facing each other; on the left was a fountain with a big-chested imitation of the "Little Mermaid" of Copenhagen sitting in the middle. Only a lone vulture, perched on

her head, seemed to strike a sinister note.

"Tomokato!" came a woman's musical voice. "Welcome, good sir knight!"

On the far side of the yard, beneath a lofty pointed archway, stood a tall blond lady clad all in white samite, holding aloft a bright torch and attended by several maids. Tomokato made toward them, expecting the trap to be sprung at any moment.

"I am Morgan Le Fairchilde," the Lady called. "You have had a hard journey. I pray you will tarry here awhile and accept our hospitality."

"I seek the Spad," Tomokato said, dismounting. "Where is it?"

"All in good time, sir knight," the Lady replied with a lovely smile. Indeed, of all the human females he had ever seen, she was by far the most beautiful.

"I won't be stayed from my course," Tomokato said.

"I doubt it not," she replied, and directed one of her maids to take his horse. "We have no use for the Spad; you may have it, and good riddance."

"Really?" Tomokato asked. "I thought you wanted to protect your son from it."

"You mean Mordred?" she asked. "I could not care less about the little toad. He never writes."

"If you try to trick me, you'll regret it," Tomokato warned. "Even my respect for your brother won't save you."

"Ahh, Arthur," she said. "Is he well? He doesn't write either. Of course, the posts *are* irregular here."

"I can imagine. Take me to the Spad."

"First let us feast you, at least. We have been so long without guests." Tomokato thought he detected a lascivious note in the words, but her expression gave no hint of it. "Follow me, Sir Tomokato."

"Wait!" he growled, but she and her maids were already through the archway. He could have seized and threatened her, but he wanted to find out just what her game was. Perhaps she might even lead him to the plane, if only to raise his hopes and then crush them. She plainly

enjoyed playing with her victims.

He started into the corridor, but before going too far, stopped and looked back toward the gatehouse. The portcullis was down, and the vulture was roller-skating ominously in the court-yard, followed by a train of rats carrying small coffins. Turning, the cat headed forward once more.

The corridor was clean and brightly lit, dec-orated with magnificent tapestries depicting what Tomokato guessed was the story of Joseph of Arimathea flying the Spad to Britain. At the end the cat found himself in a vast banquet-hall, a table in the middle covered with cloth of gold and set for two. Morgan Le Fairchilde beck-oned him over to it.

"Make yourself at home, good knight," she said. "My maids are at your beck and call."

"Here, My Lord," one said. "Let me make you more comfortable." She made as if to take Tomokato's swordbelt off; gently but firmly, he pushed her soft hand aside.

"As you wish, My Lord," she said bowing, and withdrew.

Morgan Le Fairchilde showed him a mock-ing smile. "You'll have to take it off if you want to sit at the table," she said, settling into a tall carven chair.

He eyed her narrowly, remaining motionless.

"You're so mistrustful," the Lady said. "We mean you no harm. We wish only to give you pleasure."

"Like the water-maidens?" he asked.

Morgan laughed. "You'll be served no Reese's Pieces here." At a nod from her, two serving-maids laid an electrum platter of Godiva choco-lates on the table before him. "And if you want video . . ." She flipped open a panel on the arm of her chair, revealing a brace of electronic con-trols, and pressed a button; a huge video screen slid up from the floor, twenty feet on a side, showing a geriatric Harrison Ford snuggling up to an equally ancient Carrie Fisher against a background of stars and careening spaceships.

"A bootleg of *The Jedi's Big Score*," Morgan announced. "The sixth *Stars Wars* flick. Very hard to come by. Lucas hasn't even made the movie yet."

Tomokato said nothing.

"Do you like cocaine?" Morgan asked, producing a huge bag of it out of nowhere and scooting it across the table toward the cat.

"I understand it's bad for the sinuses," he replied.

"Actually, I've got some industry spokesmen in the other room that vigorously deny that." Morgan pressed another button, summoning them into the hall—a crowd of very sharply dressed, obviously Colombian types.

"Drugs are for weaklings," Tomokato said sternly.

Morgan banished the spokesmen back to their chamber. "Well then, Sir Tomokato," she said, "perhaps you're more interested in fleshly delights." The neckline of her gown suddenly plunged, and her lips developed a fatal crimson gloss; leaning forward to show off her décolletage, she whispered huskily, "Stay with me. Abandon your quest. Love me forever."

"Even if I could abandon my quest," Tomokato said, "you and I could never be happy."

"How do you know?"

"We're too different. You're not—Japanese."

"Don't let that worry you. I'm kinky."

"And I've given up the pleasures of the flesh."

Morgan bit her lip, exasperated by his moral fortitude. "Well, what about those chocolates then?"

"Enough of this," Tomokato announced. "You said you'd take me to the Spad."

"You rancid little prig!" Morgan spat, clearly losing her temper. "I only hinted I would." She pointed a long-nailed finger at him. "He's all yours, girls!"

There came a hail of footbeats, and Tomokato turned to see a horde of Morgan's maids closing on three sides, transforming into leprous hags even as they came, whirling *nunchakus* and razor-edged scythes.

"You don't have any monopoly on Zen here, Tomokato!" Morgan cried. "Had 'em all trained in Okinawa when I heard you were coming!"

Tomokato dashed to the right along the table, sword out, slashing, boning whole bodies with single strokes; geysering scarlet, hags spun to the floor. Ripping through the tightening semicircle, Tomokato pivoted after a few yards, turning on the hags charging in from behind. Steel whining through the blood-misted air, he sheared rib cages like a demonic Dr. De Bakey, sent severed heads bouncing across the floor like beach balls of the damned; *nunchakus* and

scythes dropped from nerveless fingers. A few murderous seconds more and the last of Morgan's henchwomen were dispatched to the Haggy Hunting Ground.

Only then did he notice the metamorphosis the hall had undergone—the pink stone walls had darkened to a slime-coated black, water dripped from the vaulted ceiling, and the tapestries hung in rotted tatters; the cloth of gold on the table had become a jam-and-peanut-butter-clotted plastic tablecloth decorated with still-recognizable pictures of Michael Jackson, the cocaine had become tubes of airplane glue, and the Godiva chocolates had degenerated into—you guessed it—Reese's Picces. Even the movie on the video screen had changed; Harrison Ford and Carrie Fisher had been replaced by Tor Johnson and Vampira. Tomokato shuddered, confronted by *Plan Nine* itself. . . .

He looked at Morgan. She had not stirred from her seat. Still as beautiful as ever, even though her face was livid with rage, she cried:

"You're pretty good at slaughtering old women. But let's see how you do against a *real* badass!" And with that, she leaped to her feet, spreading wide her arms. Thunder smote Tomokato's ears, he watched awestruck as her face lengthened, sprouting scales, and her teeth became great curving fangs. Golden hair dropped away from her head, which swiftly developed serrate ridges and shining yellow horns. Bursting out of her white samite gown, a green-plated reptilian body doubled, tripled, quadrupled in size; her arms became leathery bat wings, her legs massive pillars of muscle. Eyes glowing a fiery orange-red, switching her spiny tail back and forth, the dragon that had been Morgan Le Fairchilde kicked the table aside with a taloned foot and advanced on the cat, maw yawning wide, a glaring hell-blaze shooting up from her throat, silhouetting her fangs for an instant before flooding downward at Tomokato.

The cat dodged aside; the floor where he had stood transformed instantly into a pool of molten rock. Retreating, he almost tripped over one of the dead hags and bounded backward over the corpse. Just missing him, the next blast struck the body, the sheer force of it rolling the corpse several yards over the floor, the cat backpedaling furiously to avoid it.

A third torrent of fire licked down at the cat, but this time he ducked beneath it, hurdled the blazing hag, and ran straight toward the dragon, slashing the monster across the leg. Hissing in agony, black blood gouting from the wound, the dragon went down on one knee, her underbelly now in reach of Tomokato's blade. A ferocious blow tore a rent in her stomach; Tomokato barely saved himself from the fire that came jetting forth, and before he could attempt another stroke, her wings began to beat, lifting her huge body up from the floor, yards out of range of his sword.

Dashing forward, he raced beneath her toward two rusty pikes crossed on the wall ahead beside a portcullised archway. Sheathing his sword, he reached one of the weapons, wrenched it from the wall, and spun.

Wings thudding, stirring hurricanelike winds, the dragon hurtled toward him, liquid flame rivering out of her gashed belly. But no more fire belched from her jaws; Tomokato guessed the stomach-wound was the reason. *Depressurized her*, he thought.

Before her saurian head could lash in at him, he hurled the pike with a mighty effort into the gale from her pinions, straight at a joint where wing met shoulder. The blade drove deep, and she dropped to the floor, staggering on her wounded leg.

Tomokato grabbed the other pike, but the monster's head darted at him even as he turned, and the fanged jaws snapped down on the weapon's head, biting it off. Racing for the nearby archway, he sped in under the portcullis, heard the thump-and-drag of the monster limping after him. Spotting the wall-mounted wheel that controlled the portcullis, he whipped his sword back out and sliced through the hoist-rope; as the spiked gate squealed down, he looked back, saw the dragon retreating, trying to jerk her head out from under—too late. Catching her neck beneath a foot-wide spike, the portcullis pinned it to the floor, the point penetrating with a black spurt. Her head jerked upward at a terrible angle, vertebrae severed.

Tomokato watched the great corpse warily, wondering if there might, impossibly, be any life left in it, or whether Morgan might change into yet another form and attack. As if to con-

firm his fears, a bluish mist rose from the dragon's mouth and swiftly coalesced into a phantasm of her original beauteous self. But it made no threatening moves; indeed, all it did was shrug resignedly and say, "So *that's* how you do against a real badass," and slide down through the floor toward the infernal regions.

Out of the corner of his eye, the cat saw a sign on the left-hand wall. Suicidal? it asked. This Way to the Spad. A red arrow pointed up the corridor. What dangers awaited him that way? He smiled slightly, knowing the question was irrelevant. He had no choice but to follow the arrow.

Turning, he started slowly up the torchlit passage, going around a bend; there was only darkness ahead. Backtracking, he plucked a torch from its socket before proceeding into the gloom.

A veritable labyrinth awaited him, dozens of branching corridors, crawl spaces, up and down escalators, on and off ramps, bicycle lanes and scenic trails. If not for the arrows, he knew he would have become hopelessly lost; and presently the arrows disappeared. He had to go on without them, sniffing the air, alert for the least hint of a Spad-like odor. But try as he might, he could not catch the telltale scent.

"Spad detectors!" he heard a voice crying presently. "Find your way to the Spad!"

Tomokato followed the sound, coming upon an old vendor dressed all in rags, with dozens of small round objects sitting on a folding table in front of him.

"Can I interest you in a Spad detector?" the vendor asked, flashing Tomokato a near-toothless smile.

"How do they work?" Tomokato asked, picking one up.

"Just like a compass. The needle'll point you straight to *this.*" The old man held up a photo of the Spad.

Might as well give it a try, Tomokato thought. "How much?"

"Twenty quid."

Tomokato forked the money over and went off with the detector. As he threaded his way in and out of one winding corridor after another, the needle, which had wavered somewhat at first, began to point more steadily; he guessed he was getting closer and closer to his goal.

The walls kept grinding inward, inexorably, remorselessly. On and on he swept through the

narrowing corridor, no side-exits and no end in sight—until his torchlight revealed a black aperture beyond which the walls did not appear to extend. He forced more speed into his strides, drawing ever closer, the walls very near to him now, almost touching his shoulders—

There sounded the snap of many hidden mechanisms being activated, and literally hundreds of inch-wide holes opened in the floor before him, sharp steel spikes eight inches long clicking up out of them. Tomokato stopped in his tracks, just on the threshold of the spikefield. He would have to tread slowly from now on. Too slowly to reach the end. . . .

Then it occurred to him that the spikes would keep the walls from closing any farther. Laughing at the stupidity of the trap's designers, he advanced cautiously among the metal fangs. The walls grated farther and farther in, but just as he had guessed, ground to a halt when they came up against the spikes.

Planting his feet unhurriedly between the skewers, he got halfway in; then the outer rows of spikes slipped back into the floor, and all at once the walls jumped in an inch to right and left, now touching his shoulder-plates. He turned sideways to give himself more room, and a stone panel slid back in front of him, revealing a red neon sign that said: Thought We Were Pretty Dumb, Didn't You?

He thought of trying to brace his torch or *katana*-blade between the walls, but realized there was no longer enough space. As fast as he could, certain it would not be fast enough, he advanced crabwise, deeper into the spike-field. Two more rows of spikes dropped back into their sockets, and the walls jerked in another two inches. He advanced another few yards. Two more braces of steel teeth vanished. The walls closed yet farther.

Not long now, he told himself.

Finally he came to a huge dusty chamber, lit with a dim, sourceless greenish glow, walls carved with gigantic images of leering gargoyles. In the middle was an area screened off with curtains.

This is the Place, read a large sign affixed to the cloth.

Tomokato advanced warily, certain he would be attacked. But he reached the front screen unmolested.

They're behind it, he thought, *waiting for me to slash my way through*. He stepped back a bit, eyeing the curtain. It would be easy to pull it over. Grabbing the cloth, he yanked the screen down, dashing to get out of its way as it fell.

But no one was inside; there was only a small folding-table, like the old vendor's. Tomokato went closer to it. There was a photo of the Spad on it. The needle of the Spad detector was pointed straight at the picture.

Off in the distance, he thought he heard what might have been an old vendor laughing his guts out.

Hurling the detector down, he left the chamber. He thought of trying to find the vendor again and getting his money back; but it was a crazy idea. And was that a faint whiff of Spad blowing in from the right?

He set off along the passage, but had not gone far when he felt one of the flagstones give slightly under his foot; there was a soft click, and moments later a far-off rumble echoed down the corridor. He paused, stepping away from the stone that had shifted, and listened.

The rumbling faded. He continued forward.

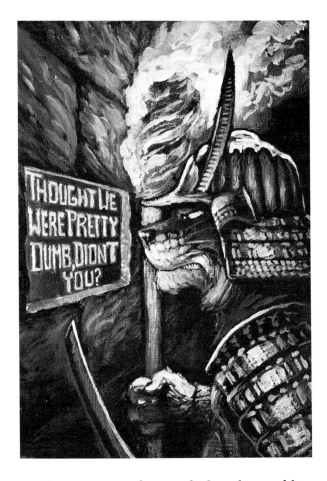

He went some distance before the rumbling began again, much closer now, mixed with a rasping grate of stone on stone. On either side the walls began creeping inward.

He looked behind, thinking to race back down the corridor, but the hall was blocked; a smooth sheet of steel had slipped noiselessly across the passage.

Forward or nothing, he thought and started to sprint.

With a jingling sound, a long pull-chain dropped out of the ceiling, dangling next to him, a note attached to the end. He took the note and read it.

Wall-switch, it said. Go on, try it.

It can't hurt at this point, he thought, and pulled the chain.

A cascade of party-streamers and confetti rained over him.

Another stone panel opened up on the wall in front of hm; this time the sign read:

Some Joke, Eh Boss?

Fury boiled up in him, but he fought it,

trying to think. A question flashed into his head: Were the walls and this neon sign on the same circuit?

Yet another two rows of spikes retracted. The walls almost reached his chest and back. The next time he would be pinned, and the time after that, the crushing would begin.

He raised his sword. Its hilt was fully insulated; more than once he had had to carve up enemy electronics in the service of his Lord Nobunaga. With its tip he pried the sign's plug from its socket, then thrust the point deep into the socket itself. A shower of sparks jetted out as the circuit shorted and his blade hummed; the neon letters sputtered into darkness. The rumbling of the walls ceased.

He breathed a deep sigh of relief.

Even so, sure as he was that the walls were completely out of commission, he worked his way out from between them as quickly as possible.

Ahead lay a high, wide corridor. This one, however, was mercifully short, ending after a dozen yards or so at an open doorway with the words *Spad Chapel* graven above it. Going through, the cat finally found himself in sight of his objective.

The plane stood in a strange chamber that could best be described as a high gothic Quonset hut, with hangar doors at one end. Unlike most of the Spads the cat had seen, this one was covered in gold foil and dotted with gems of all kinds, though it still bore the rondelles of the Roman Air Force.

Between Tomokato and the plane were two last potential obstacles: a ten-foot-tall ogre in a security-guard outfit, a double-bladed axe at its belt, and a middling-sized man very much in need of a shave, wearing a leather coat and a weather-beaten fedora, one hand on a long wet towel slung over his shoulder. There seemed to be something both archetypally pulp-adventurish and vaguely archaeological about him. The two did not seem to be aware of the cat; spaced twenty feet apart, they stood facing each other as if for a shoot-out.

Without warning, the ogre went for its axe, hurling it underhand.

The man whipped the towel from his shoulder and snapped it out at the axe, knocking it from midair.

Howling, the ogre charged forward, flashing a buck-knife out of a sheath on its wrist. The adventurer rushed to meet the creature, lashed his towel into the ogre's midsection, doubling the monster over, then whipped a dent the size of Dom DeLuise in the monster's forehead. The ogre dropped face down, dead.

"Neatly done," said the cat, approaching.

"Thank you," the man said, slinging his towel back over his shoulder. "You after the Spad?"

Paw on hilt, Tomokato halted a short distance from him and nodded.

"This is going to cause problems," the man said.

"It needn't," Tomokato answered. "Just let me have the plane."

"I'm afraid I can't do that. I was hired to—er, *procure* it for the University of Delaware Air Force ROTC, and I've already taken an advance."

"Pity," Tomokato said.

"Yeah. Pity—"

"Look out!" Tomokato broke in as a second security-ogre, brandishing a mace, came hurtling toward the man out of a security-ogre hidey-hole. Whirling, the adventurer took it out with a single snap of his terrycloth weapon.

"Guess I owe you one, cat," he said.

"I think so," Tomokato said.

"Well," the other began, "maybe we can settle this without bloodshed. What's your name?"

"Miaowara Tomokato."

"I've heard of you. Folks call me Wisconsin Platt."

"I've heard of you, too," Tomokato said respectfully.

"Why do you want the Spad?"

"It's the only way I can exact vengeance on a man who helped slay My Lord."

"Nothing else will do?"

"Not according to the Prophecy."

"Prophecy? It wouldn't have anything to do with killing Prince Mordred, would it?"

"Yes."

Platt grinned. "Wouldn't mind watching him get strafed into oblivion. Him and his whole damned army, in fact."

"You have a score to settle, too?"

"His troops made my life hell on the way here. Captured me once. Mordred himself was going to do the honors with a hot brand, but I managed to escape. If you'll let me have the Spad when you're through with him, I think a side trip to knock him off wouldn't be such a bad idea. Among other things, we'd be doing this island a big favor."

"I'm glad we can work together," Tomokato said.

"Came through the maze, eh?" Platt asked.

"Yes. Is there another way?"

"Absolutely—guided tours, twice daily. I came in with a bunch of your countrymen, as a matter of fact. While they were popping away with their flashbulbs, I slipped off from the group and hid in the men's room. Came out after closing."

"Very clever."

"Thank you. Let's get those hangar doors open."

Once that was done, Platt got into the Spad's cockpit; Tomokato revved the prop before joining him.

"Twin-seater," Tomokato said, settling down next to the adventurer. "Unusual."

"This was a special model for the Judean Procurator's Motor Vehicle Department," Platt replied. "The Saducees and Pharisees used to take their flying exams in it. Had to be room for the grader."

"Saducees and Pharisees?" Tomokato mused. "No Zealots?"

"Are you kidding? Pontius Pilate giving flying licenses to Zealots? Might as well give 'em to Germans or Parthians."

"I see your point."

Pulling the Spad through the hangar doors, Platt accelerated along a stone runway that had been built out over a sheer mountain slope. Lifting off just before reaching the end, he steered west, then south over the crags and gloomy valleys of Magorant, toward the Northumbrian border.

Tomokato turned his gaze to the dashboard. Attached to it was a plastic figure of the Blessed Virgin. Noticing some handwriting on its base, he looked closer, reading: "To Joseph of Arimathea, all the best, Mary."

Bet that's worth a fortune, he thought.

His eyes wandered to the glove compartment, and he reached toward it. But all at once Platt cried:

"Don't touch that!"

"Why not?"

"You see that lettering on the front?"

"Yes, but I can't read it."

"It's in Aramaic, the language of first-century Palestine. It says, 'Do Not Open If You've Got Any Smarts—Celestial Light and Magic Corporation.'"

"Celestial Light and Magic?" Tomokato asked.

"God's own special effects company. That compartment's full of the deadliest visuals ever devised by the Almighty. The nastiest things you've seen in the movies are just pale reflections. If you open that compartment and you're not wearing the right kind of glasses, you're dead meat. You and everyone for a couple miles around."

"And what are the right kind of glasses?"

"One green lens, one red," Platt replied. "Like these." He produced a pair of paper 3-D spectacles. "Picked 'em up when I went to see *Comin' At Ya.*"

"That was a very bad movie," Tomokato said gravely.

Platt nodded in agreement. "That bit with the baby's butt—Good Lord, right into the camera lens."

Suddenly Tomokato realized that he, too, had a pair of 3-D specs tucked away; he had gotten them going to see *Spacehunter—Adventures in the Forbidden Zone* his last night at Camelot. Arthur and his court had a burning passion for schlocky movie gimmicks—the inside of Camelot was littered with old glasses. *Spacehunter* was Arthur's favorite 3-D flick, even though Merlin was torn between *Parasite* and *Bwana Devil.* 3-D, on the other hand, gave the cat a headache; he had only gone to be polite. Only Buddha knew why he had kept the specs.

Night came down after an hour or so. Unable to navigate in the dark, Platt landed the Spad a few miles into Northumbria, on an abandoned Roman airfield.

"You know, I've been thinking," Tomokato said as they prepared their meal, "Arthur's men have 3-D glasses. Perhaps we should simply fly back to Camelot, wait for Mordred's attack, then open the glove compartment."

"But what if Mordred already has the castle surrounded?" Platt asked. "Last I heard, his army was on the move. We don't have a radio, so we can't warn Arthur about the glasses."

"Too bad there's not room enough *inside* the walls for us to land."

"Fortunes of war," Platt said, taking his first bite of the Prince Yamato Corned Beef Hash Tomokato had supplied.

Far to the south on the following morning, a small company of Mordred's troops, led by Mordred himself, Mister Ed the Saxon, and Ali Akbar Khan, Mordred's chief East German adviser, rode up to Camelot's moat under a white flag. The water was choked with fallen siege-towers and corpses; bodies peppered with arrows were strewn thickly beside the moat in a grisly band that reached halfway around the castle. Croaking happily as they tore at dead flesh, the corbies were partying to the max, and there were a lot more than twa of them, let me tell you.

Having encircled the castle with his army the preceding day, Mordred had unleashed two massive assaults on the walls, one in the afternoon, one in the dead of night. Both had been beaten back, and Arthur had lost many of his

best knights. Mordred guessed a third attack would probably finish the defenders. Yet it was likely to be a Pyrrhic victory, and how would he keep his subject kings in line with his surviving troops all covered with pyrrh? His councillors had suggested trying to bargain Camelot out from under his father; Mordred had agreed it was worth a try.

"I have something of yours, Dad," he shouted when Arthur and Merlin appeared on the battlements. "Surrender, and I just might let you have it back." He signaled. Six knights on foot came forward, pushing a large object covered with a tarpaulin.

"What is it, if I might ask?" Arthur cried.

Laughing wickedly, Mordred reached over and yanked the tarpaulin off. Revealed was a horse spread-eagled on a rack.

"It's your faithful mount," Mordred shouted triumphantly. "Traveller!"

"Traveller's not my horse," Arthur replied. "He's Robert E. Lee's horse."

Mordred blanched. It was a few moments before he said anything. "Get outta here," he

36

answered at last.

"Want to bet?"

"It's just not true. . . ."

"Come on, big shot," Arthur laughed. "Put your money where your mouth is."

"Don't bet," said Ali Akbar Khan, riding up beside Mordred. "I think my men may have grabbed the wrong animal."

As if to prove the East German's point, Robert E. Lee strode in angrily from the left and planted himself in front of Mordred.

"Will you give me my horse back, suh?" he asked gratingly.

"Release the beast," Mordred snapped to the knights by the rack, and they cut Traveller down. Saddling up, Lee wheeled him round and started off in the direction of Virginia.

But suddenly, with a howl of rage, Mordred unshouldered an AKM assault-rifle and sprayed horse and rider full of holes.

"Lord Mordred," said Ali Akbar Khan, "please try to control yourself. They've got newsmen up on the walls, action-cams. Remember Stalin's First Law: Never kill *anyone* in front of a camera—"

"Bastard!" Mordred snarled. "This is all your fault!" Turning the Kalashnikov on him, he hosed the East German off his steed in a burst of vaporized blood.

"*Jesu Christus*, you're a jerk!" cried Arthur from the battlements. "Must've gotten it all from your mother's side of the family."

"Sneer at me all you like, Father!" Mordred yelled. "We'll be coming for *you* now! And when we're done with Camelot, there won't be a living soul inside!"

"Better than living under your damned Industrial Policy!" Arthur roared.

"Industrial Policy's only the beginning!" Mordred replied. "After that, it'll be a value-added tax, wage and price controls, free coinage of silver, William Jennings Bryan, giant free cheeses in the White House . . ."

"The White House hasn't been built yet!"

"Then I'll build one of my own, somewhere where the climate's even muggier and nastier than Washington!"

"You're nuttier than a fruitcake!" Arthur cried.

"Yeah," Mordred jeered. "And I've got a much bigger army than one, too."

With that, he and his company rode back toward his lines. Once he was out of bowshot,

the flag of truce went down; raising his AKM on high, he bellowed: "Attack! Kill them all! *No quarter!*"

Horns blared, and his army pushed forward, Czech-built siege-towers leading the way, driven by oxen concealed in their bases. Withering clouds of arrows sang down from Camelot as Mordred's forces came in range, streaking between the armored towers, killing the attackers by the hundreds; but there was no way of stopping the towers themselves, and soon they were at the moat. Assault-bridges came cranking down, wide enough for ten men abreast. Climbing up through the towers, Mordred's crack shock troops, Saxons of the Remember Mount Badon Brigade, poured across the spans behind several ranks of classic Germanic shieldwall, keeping their momentum despite the archers pouring fire into them from the front. As the bowmen died, knights and men-at-arms with sword and shield took their places, hammering at the Saxons. All along the walls of Camelot, it was hand-to-hand on a titanic scale. Weapons and shields shattered. Blood splashed. Bodies crumpled.

Arthur and his men fought with ferocious courage and determination. Several of the siege-towers were pulled over with grappling-lines, and for a time it seemed as though the attack might be thrown back.

But then the Saxon footholds on the walls began to widen, and Mordred hurled in his Bulgarians and North Koreans and Magyars and Tatars and Aztecs and Zulus; the battle began to turn horribly against the defenders.

Yet just as defeat seemed certain, a gold-glinting shape came flying over the hills to the north, and roared toward the carnage. A cry rose up from the defenders, "The Spad! The Spad!" Mordred's soldiers were seized with dread.

With a staccato flash and rattle of two wrathful Vickers machine guns, the plane swooped low over the assault-bridges, ripping into the wood with phosphorus-laden bullets. Corpses flew, and splinters and flame, and the bridges went up one after another, running with fire, cutting off the flow of reinforcements from the ground.

Unable to make good their losses now, Mordred's soldiers on the wall were in a hopeless predicament; the Spad made another pass, strafing the troops near the base of the towers,

sending long spurts of bullet-torn earth skyward, spinning riddled victims to the ground. Soon Mordred's army was in headlong retreat.

Looking out over the side of the cockpit, Tomokato tapped Platt on the shoulder and pointed. "Look! Mordred's banner!"

"All *right!*" Platt said with relish, steering down toward the black-and-crimson flag. "I think I see him—yeah! Black horse, black cape—he's so damn melodramatic!"

Coming in low, guns spitting death into a churning sea of troops, they saw Mordred pitch from the saddle as the slugs ripped by; but Platt loosed two fifty-pound bombs just to make sure.

"I'll double back, see if I got him," Platt said, and swerved the Spad round.

"Wisconsin," Tomokato said, eyeing the battlements of Camelot, "I think Arthur's men are all . . ." He shook his head in disbelief, pulling out a pair of binoculars to take a better look. "They've all got their 3-D glasses on! How is it possible? . . ."

"Thinking of opening the compartment?" Platt cried, steering back toward Mordred's host now. "Forget it. If Mordred's dead, Arthur and crew can handle the rest of 'em. No point unleashing such a force unless we have to—"

"But Mordred's alive!" Tomokato broke in.

It was unmistakable; sable cloak bellying in the wind, surrounded by a waste of corpses, Mordred stood atop the body of his horse, waving his tattered banner defiantly in one hand, AKM in the other. Even above the sound of the Spad's engine, Tomokato heard him thundering:

"Top o' the world, Ma! Top o' the world!"

"Son of a bitch," gritted Wisconson Platt, and started firing. Two long strings of dusty bullet-impacts chewed up the earth, heading straight for Mordred . . .

And then the ammo ran out.

Tomokato caught a sound like an IBM Selectric going full steam—Mordred's gun. Suddenly a hail of slugs came ripping up through the Spad's fuselage; flame burst from under the cowling, a crimson spurt leaped from Platt's shoulder, and a tremendous shock set the inside of Tomokato's helmet ringing like a bell. The cat tried to stay conscious, but an inner voice whispered that the bullet had gone clear through his skull, and he might as well give up. The dubiousness of this argument was immediately ap-

41

parent to him; how could he still be thinking if his brains were blown out? His inner voice could have come back with some kind of mind-body dualist answer, but even if such an answer had occurred to it, it whispered nothing further.

Hah, Tomokato thought.

And blacked out anyway.

He woke soaking wet with the sooty smell of damp smoke in his nostrils, blood leaking down his face where the bullet had grazed him. The Spad was folded up horribly against the bole of an oak. Where all the water had come from, he could only guess; but earlier he had glimpsed a small pond from the air—the Spad had probably skidded in across it, the fires under the cowling doused just before the plane smacked into the tree.

He looked over at Platt. The adventurer was slumped in his seat, eyes closed; but he was breathing. Even as the cat looked at him, he reached up to feel the bullet wound in his shoulder. Groaning, wincing, he opened his eyes.

"Just look at that front end," he said, squinting at the crumpled metal before them. "Good thing we were wearing our seat belts. Air bag would've been nice, too." He rubbed the back of his neck. "Think I've got whiplash. How about you?"

"We've got worse problems," Tomokato said, looking past him at the mob of Saxons sweeping their way. Turning to the right, he saw an even thicker throng. Only one hope now: the glove compartment.

"Wisconsin, put your 3-D glasses on!" he said, reaching for his.

"Now where did I stick 'em. . . ." Platt searched frantically through his pockets.

"Wisconsin . . ." Tomokato grated, watching them come, wondering if he should just leap out of the cockpit, pull his sword free, and wade into them. . . .

"Got 'em!" Platt cried, putting his specs on.

Tomokato's paw darted toward the compartment—

"Got what?" Mordred demanded, leaping onto the bottom wing and pressing the muzzle of the AKM into the side of Tomokato's face.

"Oh, nothing," Tomokato replied, sagging back.

"Shall we torture them now?" asked Mister Ed, shouldering his way through his Saxon

underlings.

"Well, we can start, at least," Mordred answered, pulling a lit propane torch out from under his mailshirt.

Think fast, Tomokato, the cat told himself.

Beside him, a Saxon blade under his chin, Platt was delighted to see a phantasmal light bulb wink on above Tomokato's head.

"What does that light bulb mean?" Mordred snarled.

"To me, it means progress," said Mister Ed. "Human advancement. The end of the dark ages, the beginning of the Electrical Era—"

"Shut up," said Mordred, turning the flame up on the torch.

"Do whatever you like to me," Tomokato said, "but please, I beg you, don't hurt my pet turtle Musashi."

"Where is he?" Mordred asked, leering evilly.

"In the glove compartment."

"Right," said Mordred. And handing the blowtorch to Mister Ed, he opened the compartment.

There was an instant of low, threatening humming; then yellow light flooded forth, two thin, braided streams of it shooting directly into

Mordred's eyes. He began to glow from within, and his teeth crackled with lightning, and he flung away the AKM, leaning up against the upper wing of the plane, arms outstretched on either side.

"Shit," he said.

And having established him as a conduit, the glove compartment of the Holy Spad went awesomely to town.

Bolts of seething varicolored energy shot from his fingertips, flying in every direction; within seconds the air for miles around was thick with a whirling storm of it, a marvel of effects animation. And out of that storm, more terrible, more tangible effects began to coalesce, reflections of the Divine Visuals only one metaphysical level removed from the mind of the Ultimate Effects Man himself, the being of whom even Ray Harryhausen was but a faint adumbration. Down upon Mordred's army came the wrath of a King Kong that never looked even once like an eighteen-inch-high model, a Beast From Twenty Thousand Fathoms that seemed to have been animated by the guys that did *Dragonslayer*, a *Ten Commandments* Red Sea without a trace of matte-lines, clapping horrendously shut over a thousand Bulgarians; monsters by the score ripped into Saxons and East Germans and traitorous British knights, dealing out deaths so realistic that even Dick Smith would've vomited. Always a great Godzilla fan, Tomokato was intensely gratified to see the big guy stomping bodies in rare form, plainly relishing the fact that he was not being embodied by a little fellow in a rubber costume.

As for Mordred, a hideous prosthetic transformation sequence had taken possession of him; his lightning-shot eyes bulged from their sockets like bladders full of air, and his nose and jaws pushed out into a hairy werewolf snout. Tremendous bloated veins swelled at his temples, and his scalp developed a monstrous second face, as though *The Thing From Another World*—John Carpenter's version, not Howard Hawks'—was trying to bust out through the top of his head.

But all at once the lightning emanating from his fingers began to shoot backward into his hands. Dissolving, diffusing, the corporeal effects changed back into glowing celestial plasma, taking with them the bodies of their victims, sucking the field clean like unearthly Electroluxes;

and as the last vestiges of the energy-storm swept back into Mordred's flesh, his grotesquely-transformed skull exploded in a splashing, slow-motion flurry of crimson fragments.

Yet even that was not the end. As the yellow light faded back into the glove compartment, Mordred and all his various flying bits were inhaled into the opening, like smoke into a vacuum cleaner, with a truly cosmic slurping noise; then, with awesome finality, the compartment banged shut with a heavy thud loud out of all proportion to the door's size, as if God Himself had decreed: " 'Nuff said."

Tomokato and Platt looked slowly at each other, awestruck. Then they unhooked their seat belts and rose, gazing out over the surrounding landscape. Not a single trace of Mordred's army remained.

Above them, sitting on an oak bough, a bluebird started singing something that sounded suspiciously like *Zip-A-Dee-Doo-Dah*.

Later that day, beside the Round Table, Tomokato asked Arthur how his men had known to wear their glasses.

"Merlin said it might be a good idea," the king replied. "He knew about the glove compartment and guessed you might try to use it. So when the Spad showed up, we ordered everyone to put their specs on."

"Some show," said Merlin.

"It was so nice seeing Godzilla being done properly," said Lancelot.

"It was indeed," agreed Tomokato.

"And what about you, Wisconsin?" Arthur asked, turning to Platt. "What will they say at the University of Delaware when you show up empty-handed? Can you return the advance?"

"No need to," the adventurer said, and jerked a thumb toward Sir Gawaine. "Gawaine here tells me there's a Spad repair shop just a few klics down the road. I expect they'll be able to cobble it back together—"

Shouts and hurrying footsteps; a page rushed into the chamber, knelt before Arthur, and said:

"Terrible news, My Lord!"

"Out with it," Arthur said.

"The Argentines," the page answered breathlessly. "They've invaded the Falklands."

Arthur slapped a hand to the back of his neck, swearing under his breath. "If it isn't one damn thing, it's another. Last thing I need now is to lead an expeditionary force . . ."

"Well," said Merlin, "with Sir Tomokato on our side, we should do well enough."

"Sorry," Tomokato said. "I can't go with you."

"But you're one of my knights," Arthur answered.

"Before I entered your service, I served another, and too many of his slayers are still alive."

Arthur opened his mouth to reply, but Merlin said hurriedly:

"Sire, perhaps Tomokato *has* done you service enough. In most versions of this story, the Round Table falls apart, you get killed, and the economy goes to hell in a handbasket."

"True, true," Arthur admitted. "Very well, Sir Tomokato, you may leave us. And our blessings go with you."

"Thank you, Sire," Tomokato said, and bowed.

"Are you going to leave Camelot right away?" Platt asked him.

"Yes, why?"

"Well, if you stick around till the Spad's repaired, I might be able to give you a lift."

Tomokato laughed. "Could you take me to Mars?"

"No, but I could do the next best thing—drop you off in New Jersey."

Tomokato wrinkled his nose; even in sixteenth-century Japan, there were sinister rumors of that far-off place. "How would that help?"

"Jersey's been invaded by Martians. Perhaps you could catch one of their supply ships on the return leg."

"Hmmm . . . not a bad idea."

"So you'll be staying for a bit, Tomokato?" Arthur asked.

"I think so."

"Splendid! I've got just the film. Came in yesterday morning, but we didn't have time to watch, as you might expect."

"Sire," Merlin said, "we have preparations to make. Putting together a task force is going to be very difficult. The Falklands are—"

"Come on," Arthur broke in. "We haven't seen this flick, Merlin."

"What's it called?"

Metalstorm.

"*Metalstorm*," Merlin repeated, savoring the sound of it.

Great Buddha in Heaven, thought Tomokato.

47

II. A Fighting Cat of Mars

Upon arriving in the Garden State, Tomokato learned, much to his annoyance, that the Martians were not in the least bit interested in doing business with him, or anyone else for that matter; remaining hidden in their mammoth walking war-machines, they spent their time taking pot-shots at any earthling who approached. Their forces were more than a match for New Jersey's (the Jersey Generals were absolutely helpless), but abruptly, for no apparent reason, they pulled back into their landing-ships and left the earth—with Tomokato a stowaway. Once inside, he got his first glimpse of the Martians—hideous octopoid creatures, not the red-skinned humans he had been expecting—and realized he might be heading for the wrong Mars. But the navigator, like the rest of the Martians aboard, was dying of a terminal cold and sent the ship hurtling off course—which brought the cat to his desired destination after all. . . .

—Cat Out of Hell

It was a hundred and forty miles across the dead-sea bottom from P'tang, the Martian "City of Sound Effects," that Tomokato caught up with the pilgrim-caravan he had been tracking; dead red-Martian pilgrims lay scattered by the dozens over the ochre moss, their corpses stripped of all harnesses and ornaments, their chariot-wains looted, their draught-animals, or pziditi-tars, stolen. As for who had committed this atrocity, the answer was plain enough—sprawled among the other corpses were ten or so green-skinned, three-armed giants. These creatures were known as the Four-Eyed Men, because of the Coke-bottle-lensed glasses they all wore; they were also called Green Meanies, or Emerald Dufuses, or even, Those Jerks; but never to their faces. Why they didn't mind being called Four-Eyed, Tomokato couldn't fathom, but there was much that was strange on this planet known to its natives as Bazoom.

He got down off his small pthote, a six-legged Martian steed, and searched among the bodies, comparing the faces of the male pilgrims to the photo he had clipped out of an old *Newsweek*. It was a long, tedious job, but finally he was convinced that the Green Meanies had not cheated him of his revenge—Zad Fnark, the Martian Master Assassin who had played such a cruel role in the killing of Nobunaga, was not among the slain. Which left only two possibilities: either he had escaped, or he had been carried off by the Four-Eyed Men. The latter seemed more likely.

Tomokato got back on his pthote and followed the trail of the marauders. A wide swath of the spongy yellow pturf had been crushed flat by the passing of many huge war-pthotes. The spoor led the same way the caravan had been going—east, toward the river Bliss.

Martian religion held that the Bliss was the "River of Immortality"; flowing beneath the sacred Hartz Mountains, it led to the fabled "Eden of Bazoom," a place where life-weary Martian pilgrims would find eternal joy under the rule of Mrs. Blissus, the Goddess of Everlasting Life. The pilgrimage was promoted by the Priests of Blissus, guys in bird-hats who called themselves the Holy Pterns; but why anyone would work up any confidence in folks who wore such asinine-looking headgear and smiled so greasily and sweated so much was quite beyond Tomokato. Especially when the pilgrims had to give up a huge proportion of their possessions and lands to the Pterns before they could even get a

ticket to go on the journey, and no one had ever returned to say whether they had gotten their money's worth. Tomokato had no qualms about the idea of a paradisal afterlife; but he had been suspicious of earthly paradises ever since hearing from his brother Shimura that Epcot Center wasn't all it was cracked up to be. And earthly paradises from which no postcards came were even more dubious propositions, in Tomokato's book.

The Green Meanies' spoor led the cat up the sloping eastern bank of the sea-bottom and into an ancient abandoned city that had been a port before the sea dried up. Flanked by crumbling houses and ruined palaces, the streets were full of dirt and dust. As night approached, the trail took him into the courtyard of a huge fortified structure. Red light shone through its windows and doorways. A great herd of war-pthotes and pzidititars was gathered at the far end of the yard, five Green Meanies tending them; a stone wall much overgrown with moss loomed up behind.

Tomokato rode straight across the courtyard. The Four-Eyed Men were plainly aware of him, but made no move for their weapons, going calmly about their business, feeding the animals.

"I wish to speak to your chief," the cat said.

"Inside," one grunted, jerking a clawed thumb toward a door.

Tomokato dismounted and, keeping an eye on the Green Meanies, tied his beast to a weathered stone ring protruding from the wall. Then he went under the arch, paw on hilt.

Inside the torchlit hall were at least sixty Four-Eyed Men, squatting on the sunken floor in a ring around two central pillars. Tied to one of the pillars was a gorgeous red-Martian woman, near-nude after the fashion of gorgeous red-Martian women. Tied to the other was Zad Fnark.

"Come closer, stranger!" cried a Green Meanie, rising. "Give us a good look at you!"

Tomokato went down the steps and toward them.

"Yes, into the circle!" said the giant who had spoken, motioning one of his fellow monsters aside. "I am Porquas Erntpt, Jad of the Wazoo Horde. Who are you, and what do you want?"

"I am Miaowara Tomokato," said the cat. He pointed to Zad Fnark. "I've come for that man."

"Ho! Ho! Ho!" laughed the green giant.

"What if we don't want to give him to you? After all, he's *our* prisoner—just as you are."

With that, the other Green Meanies got to their feet with a clatter of harnesses and accoutrements.

Tomokato sighed. "Why not just let me have him?" he asked. "I've no quarrel with you."

"Well, actually," said Porquas Erntpt, going back by Zad Fnark, "we've no quarrel with *him*." And in a flash he drew a knife and sliced through the red Martian's bonds. Zad Fnark reached up and pulled off his gag, sneering triumph at Tomokato.

"I hope you enjoy dying as much as you enjoy killing," the assassin said.

Tomokato's first impulse was to attack then and there; but he could not allow that remark to pass unrefuted.

"I do *not* enjoy killing," Tomokato said. "I take my satisfaction from doing my duty, and—"

"Ooh, sanctimonious, aren't we?" Zad Fnark broke in, and dashed behind the pillar. In that moment, Tomokato realized that his desire to clarify had probably cost him his quarry.

Whipping out his blade, he charged after the assassin. But the Green Meanies were already rushing in on all sides, Porquas Erntpt looming up right in front of him, striking out with an eight-foot-long sword.

Tomokato bounded up, over the blow; the lower Martian gravity allowed his muscles to propel him far higher and farther than he could ever have gone on Earth, and to Porquas Erntpt's absolute astonishment, the cat landed on the giant's shoulders, feet on either side of his head.

Other Green Meanies closed in. Tomokato jumped again, an instant before their blades came lashing down. Dying, Porquas Erntpt sank floorward, cursing his followers feebly as they tried to pull their swords out of his head.

Landing, Tomokato still had to contend with the Green Meanies whose swords were still free. They were splendid fighters, and it was only his earthly muscle-power that enabled him to polish them off in a respectably short time.

He turned back to the ones with their swords still jammed in Porquas Erntpt's skull. Grunt and strain as they might, they were having no luck. He decided to ignore them, looking about for Zad Fnark. But the assassin was nowhere to be seen. There were many exits from the hall;

which one had Zad Fnark fled through?

"Kill him!" came the assassin's voice suddenly, and Tomokato spun to see the five Green Meanies who had been feeding the war-pthotes rushing down from the doorway. Guessing Zad Fnark must be in the courtyard, Tomokato leaped over the giants to the stairhead behind, dashing outside. Mounted on Tomokato's pthote, Zad Fnark was speeding toward the gate through the deepening dusk, laughing uproariously.

"*Mothra Isuzu!*" gritted the cat in cold rage. For a few moments he stood there watching the assassin escape; then he leaped high in the air as the five Green Meanies rushed back out again. Swearing, they looked up to see him dropping back down toward them, sword wheeling; four mega-splats and a crimson shlorp later, they were stretched out on the flagstones, wondering briefly before their lights went out if they had just stuck their faces into a whirling airplane propeller.

Wiping his blade on a green giant's arm, Tomokato considered trying to mount one of the huge war-pthotes; but he had heard that the giant pthotes, once broken, would only allow

their masters to ride them—and would fight anyone else until he, or the pthote, was dead. He decided not to risk it.

"Help!" called the red-Martian woman from inside the hall. "Help me, please!"

Knowing Zad Fnark would get a good lead on him in any case, Tomokato went back in to free her. Approaching her, giving a wide berth to the Green Meanies who were still trying to yank their swords free, Tomokato saw that she had managed to work her gag down over her chin.

"May Mrs. Blissus bless you!" she said as he unfettered her. He started back toward the doorway. She ran along behind, asking breathlessly: "How can I thank you?"

"Don't mention it," he answered. Pausing beside the struggling Four-Eyed Men, he inquired: "How long do you think you gentlemen will be at this?"

One looked back over his shoulder, glasses sliding down his face. "Oh, I guess we'll be another two hours at least," he said, pushing them back up. "You guys might as well go on ahead."

"Thank you," said Tomokato. He and the red woman left the hall, but halted in the courtyard.

"Are you going after Zad Fnark?" she asked.

"I am. And I'll have him, too. He blew cigarette smoke in My Lord Nobunaga's face all the while my Master's head was being sawed off."

"Well, if you want to catch him, we'd better take one of those war-pthotes."

"We?"

"He's bound for the river Bliss and Paradise. So am I. You can protect me, at least part of the way. And I can control those pthotes."

"How?"

"I was raised by pthotes. My parents abandoned me in that big safari park outside P'tang. You know the one?"

"Passed it on my way here."

"Anyway, I know just what to say to the big old huggy-bears. Come on."

They went over to the closest brute. The monster rose up at their approach and snarled menacingly, whereupon the woman began to chant:

"Big old pthotie-poo,
Don't hurt me.
Let us ride upon your back,
Whee, whee, whee."

Lowering itself back to the flags, the creature let her climb aboard. Tomokato started to follow, then thought of something and went back to the Green Meanies he had slaughtered by the door, going through the various pouches on their harnesses. On the third body he found what he was looking for: pilgrim tickets, looted from people in the caravan. They were very valuable items—there was a huge black market for them back in P'tang.

He returned to the pthote and clambered up. The woman coaxed the beast to its feet and guided it from the courtyard with gentle kicks.

"What did you take?" she asked Tomokato.

"Pilgrim tickets," he answered. "I figured they might come in handy."

"What are you, a scalper?"

"No. I just want to make sure Zad Fnark doesn't escape me. Even if he gets to Paradise." He handed her one of the tickets. "Yours was stolen, wasn't it?"

"Yes," she said. "Thanks."

"What's your name?" Tomokato asked.

"Effluvia," she replied.

"What were you doing with Zad Fnark?"

"He wanted me for his own, the beast. That's why he had the Green Meanies spare my life when the caravan was attacked."

"Were they acting on some plan of his?"

"No, they came across the caravan by accident. But they'd worked for him before, it seemed. Caused a diversion for him after he assassinated some Earth-leader in a place called Dallas. They were only too glad to try and trap you for him."

Tomokato squinted through the twilight at the tracks Zad Fnark's pthote had left. "We won't be able to follow the trail much longer," he said. "It's getting dark."

"Don't worry about that. I know where you can head him off. Do you have a map?"

"Yes."

"Well, he's making for the Blissco Rental Dock in Kaol-Pectate. Even if we don't overtake him on the way, we'll get there long before he does. These big pthotes have much longer legs than the little kind. You'll get your man, and I'll hitch a ride with the first group of pilgrims that comes along."

"Why are you going on the pilgrimage at all?" Tomokato asked. "Why turn your back on the world? You're a young, beautiful woman, with your whole life ahead of you. . . . And you don't even know if this Paradise is really as wonderful as it's supposed to be."

"Blasphemy!" Effluvia retorted. "The Holy Pterns have told us everything about it. And they're the servants of Mrs. Blissus herself."

"But why do you believe them?"

"Because they wear bird-hats! And they smile so greasily and sweat so profusely!"

"Hmmm," said Tomokato.

"And anyway," Effluvia went on, "I have to make the pilgrimage if I want to be with Ptin Kan, my only true love."

"Does he love you?"

"Yes."

"Then why did he leave you?"

"Because he thought I'd been cheating on him. He knew how I grew up among the pthotes, and I *had* been seeing a lot of my old pal Ptrigger, and when Ptin Kan came to my room and found a pile of pthote-eggs in the corner, he

found that Zad Fnark had already departed on the Blissco Dock's fastest boat; they had to make do with a much slower craft.

For the next two days they sputtered upstream, outboard engine laboring; on the way they passed many pilgrim boats manned by Pterns who were returning them to Blissco. The Hartz Mountains rose over the horizon; even a hundred miles off, they appeared very near through the thin Martian atmosphere, a wall of crystalline peaks veined with streaks of gold. As the boat drew nearer and nearer to the shining rampart, Tomokato made out a huge fortified palace clinging to the barrier above the mighty cavern through which the Bliss passed under the mountains. Gradually he discerned tremendous letters carved on the wall of the structure—Welcome to Epcopt Center, they read. Suddenly even more suspicious of the Martian "Paradise" than before, he asked Effluvia:

"What does Epcopt stand for?"

"Ethereal Paradisal Community of Pterns," she replied. "Why?"

"Oh, nothing," he replied. "But I suspect you're going to find this place a real disappointment."

"Will you stop with your blaspheming?"

"For now."

The cavern-mouth loomed even closer. Thrown across the entrance was a pontoon dock with a gap in the middle; great numbers of Pterns were gathered on either side of the break, signaling incoming boats to draw up alongside the docks. Several Ptern airships rested on the water beyond, heavily manned with Ptern warriors keeping alert for some religious infraction from the pilgrims, no doubt.

Tomokato and Effluvia's craft was at the back of a heavy crush of traffic. The pilgrims ahead of them were asked to step out of their boat, show their tickets, and contribute all the possessions they had with them to the Pterns; they were allowed to keep only their next-to-nothing Martian garments. The Pterns then dispensed a second, different-colored ticket, drew the pilgrim craft behind the docks for return to Blissco, and unfolded the distinctly disposable-looking, engineless paper boats in which the pilgrims continued downstream.

At last it was Tomokato and Effluvia's turn. A priest took their boat, and they showed their tickets to the Ptern in charge.

just leaped to the wrong conclusion and . . ."

"What *were* the pthote-eggs doing in the corner?" Tomokato wondered aloud.

"I don't know," Effluvia replied, a note of acute distress in her voice. "Unless it was the Pthote-Egg Bunny."

"Pthote-Egg Bunny?" Tomokato asked skeptically.

Effluvia slapped a fist against her shapely thigh. "Why doesn't anyone *believe* me?"

Some distance from the city, after following a tortuous course through a stretch of low rocky hills to throw off pursuit, they stopped for the night, thinking they could easily make up Zad Fnark's lead the next day. But when morning came and they set off again, their pthote developed a flat; Tomokato had to stand around idly for three hours while Effluvia performed the tedious task of repairing the puncture. And when that was done, it was another two hours before they had the deflated leg blown back up—lacking a pump, they took turns puffing mightily into the valve.

Reaching Kaol-Pectate by midafternoon, they

"Now," the boss-Ptern said, "your goods."

Effluvia immediately forked over her ornaments, but Tomokato made no move.

"Your goods," the Ptern repeated to the cat.

"Tomokato, you're impossible!" Effluvia said.

"I will not surrender my weapons or armor," Tomokato said flatly.

"What need will you have for them in Paradise?" the Ptern-in-charge asked unctuously.

Tomokato smiled thinly at him. "Perhaps you might tell me."

"He's an unbeliever," Effluvia said. "I'm so embarrassed!"

"An unbeliever?" asked the boss-Ptern. "Then why do you want to enter Epcopt Center?"

Tomokato thought of an answer, but never gave it; three flying-craft had risen into view above the priest's shoulder, water dripping from their hulls, hibachis smoking sullenly on their decks.

"I thought as much!" cried a man standing in the bow of the central craft. "Orp Orvus, you fool! That's the cat I told you about!"

It was Zad Fnark.

The boss-Ptern spun. "How am I supposed to know what a cat looks like?" he replied.

Along the rails and bows of the fliers, Ptern warriors snatched up radium-rifles; Orp Orvus and his men leaped away from Tomokato.

Tomokato looked over at the pile of pilgrim goods, remembering some interesting items he had seen forked over to the priests. There they were among the lava-lamps and portable type-writers and lawn-ornament Mexicans—two Stinger antiaircraft launchers and a Wolverine P-30 submachine shotgun. Two Pterns stood between him and the weapons, swords out.

"Shinichi Chiba!" he shrieked, sweeping his own blade free, bounding toward them; two strokes, and the Pterns rocked backward, ripped abdomens bursting open like party-poppers, adding a festive, if highly reddish, touch to the scene.

The gunners on the fliers cut loose. The volley missed the cat, landing behind him, the concussion from the explosive radium shells actually aiding him, flinging him forward onto the goods-pile. Snatching up one of the Stingers, he opened out the tube and sight as the riflemen were reloading, then blasted the rocket at Zad

Fnark's craft, even though he could no longer see the assassin on it. The infrared homing system locked onto the craft's hibachi, and in an instant the flier disintegrated in a flaming explosion, bodies and debris arcing out of the fireball.

Raked by burning shrapnel, many of the gunners on the other two craft crumpled; the ones still at the rails started firing, but Tomokato ducked behind the goods-pile, the other Stinger already in his paws. The pile was massive enough to protect him for the time it took to unfold the launcher; then he popped back up and blew a second flier out of the air.

Smoking and listing from the damage it had taken in the first blast, the last flier heeled round and started off into the tunnel. To Tomokato's amazement, he saw Zad Fnark standing by the stern rail, beckoning and shouting:

"Come on, cat! Let's see how you fare in Paradise!"

Tomokato shook his head, wondering how the assassin had escaped; all he could think of was that his prey had leaped onto the other flier after seeing him pick up the Stinger. The craft had been close enough. . . .

Footbeats pounded on the dock off to the right; a crowd of Pterns was rushing toward him from the side of the cavern-mouth, blades flashing. Dropping the second launcher, he casually reached for the submachine shotgun and started in on them. The effect was drastic, to say the least; half a clip left the dock looking like a pizza-parlor floor after a pie fight.

Tomokato turned to the left. Orp Orvus's men were trying to sneak up on him, one already close enough to get burned across the forehead by the shotgun's hot barrel as Tomokato swung the gun round. The fellow's face creased into the most remarkable expression of stupid surprise Tomokato had ever seen; then the cat let him have it. Three more bursts took out the man's buddies. At last Tomokato halted, knowing there was only one shot left in the clip. Full auto-fire or no, he always counted his shots very carefully.

Only Orp Orvus was still on his feet, standing behind Effluvia, holding the point of a shortsword against her side.

"Drop the gun, or she dies!" the Ptern cried.

Tomokato took aim. "Drop the sword," he replied, "or *you* die!"

"You going to pick me off with buckshot?"

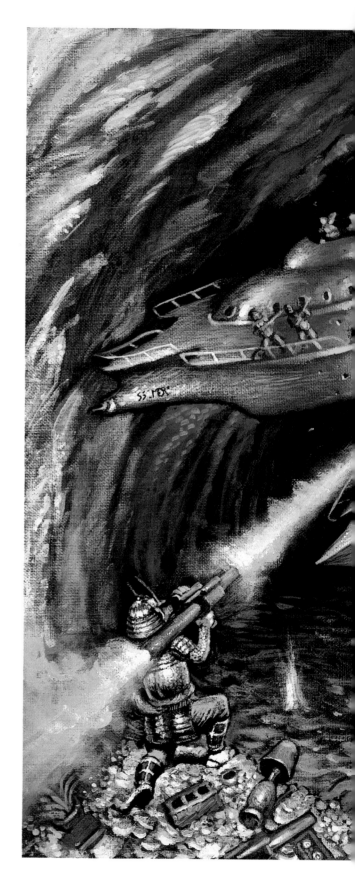

laughed the Ptern. "I'd like to see you try!"

"All right," said Tomokato, shrugging, and squeezed the trigger.

Pellet impacts peppered Orp Orvus's face and arms and legs, everything visible behind Effluvia. The Ptern dropped over the side of the dock, into the water between the halves of the pontoon barrier; Effluvia leaped forward, completely untouched.

Tomokato had aimed *very* carefully.

The cat looked over to the other side of the gap and brandished the Wolverine at a large group of Pterns there. Apparently having no idea he was out of ammo, they took off.

"Come on," he said to Effluvia, getting into a fast-looking pilgrim boat.

"With someone who murders Holy Pterns?" she demanded.

"What choice did I have? And how holy could they be if they take orders from Zad Fnark?"

"Maybe they don't know what kind of man he is!" she answered.

"Well, maybe they don't. But they're not going to take too kindly to you in any case, seeing that you came with me. You can't stay here."

"I could go back downriver."

"If you please. But you won't find Ptin Kan."

Swearing under her breath, she leaped into the boat beside him. He cast off and started up the motor, a twelve pthotepower model built under license from Evinrude; swinging the bow round, he steered straight on into the tunnel.

"Mrs. Blissus is going to *kill* us," Effluvia sulked. "I just know it."

Six hours at least they pushed downstream under the mountains, passing paper boats that had gone on before them, the way illuminated by the millions and millions of flashing multicolored Christmas tree lights that had been strung along the walls and ceiling. Set in niches were other types of Christmas decorations: reindeer-antlered plastic pthotes with red-flashing noses, bird-hatted Holy Ptern mannikins dressed in Santa suits distributing gift-wrapped packages to pilgrim mannikins, snowmen with three arms built rather like fluffy white Green Meanies. Ever since arriving on Mars, Tomokato had been struck by the way the Pterns used the more commercial kinds of yuletide images to sell their

religion. A completely secularized version of Christmas was very popular in his homeland, he knew. Was some kind of universal human principle at work here? Were all human beings suckers for jingle bells and plastic holly? If so, had these selling techniques been imported to Mars from Earth, or had they spontaneously evolved on this planet, developed in response to deep subconscious needs? If he went to other worlds, would he find such decorations? As the boat pressed on along the underground river, he devoted a good deal of thought to these matters, eventually deciding to chalk them up as some of the Eternal Mysteries. But from time to time, until his last day, he found himself haunted by these questions.

Whatever the origin of the decorative traditions, there was no doubt that they called forth quite a reaction from Effluvia; she had been very morose at the start of the underground voyage, but as it progressed her spirits rose steadily; she began whistling tunes like "Frosty the Snowman" and "Jingle Bell Rock," and was in the middle of a full-throated rendition of "Snoopy's Christmas" when Tomokato silenced her. He could see the end of the tunnel—the Christmas lights came to an abrupt end, with a starshot sky beyond. Tomokato listened as the echoes of her voice faded—he was sure he heard water rushing.

"Why'd you shush me up?" Effluvia asked, miffed. "I was really feeling fine."

"That's probably just how the Pterns want you—completely off guard. That must be what all those decorations are for: lulling everyone who comes along into a sense of false security."

"You're so damn cynical."

"I'm nothing of the sort. Now hold on to something. I think we're in for a real ride."

Effluvia laughed. "Are you talking about that rushing sound? Relax. It must be the Bliss Waterslide—The First Yet Least Thrill."

Before long they reached the end of the tunnel; there a huge metal ramp met the river, skimming off the top three feet of it. Where the rest was channeled, Tomokato had no idea. But he also had no time to think about it.

The boat teetered on the brink for an instant, then shot downward at an ever-increasing speed. The plunge seemed to last forever. Wind pummeling his face, claws dug into the bench he sat on, back pressed against the stern of the

craft, Tomokato thought to himself that this was, indeed, a thrill. And if it was the least thrill Epcopt Center had to offer, he decided he had already had his fill. Effluvia, on the other hand, seemed to be enjoying herself royally, laughing uproariously, cracking jokes about barf bags that Tomokato did not find in the least bit amusing, inviting him to join her in standing up on one foot and hopping around a bit. He almost ordered her to shut up and sit down, but the slide suddenly leveled off, then took a steep jog upward, and it was all she could do to cling to the craft as it sailed through the air and landed with a great flat-bottomed splash.

"By the gods, that was great," she declared, recovering from the impact, shouting to be heard over the sound of the waterslide. Then she hung her head over the gunwale and made a long series of boisterously unmentionable noises. "Boy," she said happily, leaning back, "I haven't thrown up like that since I was a little pthote. This *must* be Paradise!"

Tomokato steered the boat slowly forward through the darkness. He could make out two dark rows of huge trees on either side of the river, silhouetted dimly against the sky. Ahead, he saw one of Mars's two moons lifting over the rim of an ocean.

"The Lost Sea of Borus," Effluvia said, voice full of wonder.

"Why is it called that?" Tomokato asked.

"Long ago," she began, "a paperback cover artist from Earth came to this valley to vacation. He was a very vain man, always painting himself into his covers because he loved his own face and bod so much. One day, as he was looking at his reflection in a tidal pool, he leaned over to give it a hickey, but sucked up so much water that he choked to death and fell in. The sea was named after him. . . ."

Something bumped against the hull. Tomokato looked over the side; it was hard to tell, but the object slipping by to starboard seemed to be one of those disposable paper pilgrim-boats, half-sunken. After a few more minutes, they struck another, then another. Once Tomokato thought he made out the shape of a severed human hand floating in the water.

"Did you see that?" Effluvia asked.

"Yes," Tomokato replied. "You have good night vision, for a human." He cut the motor. They were by now far enough away from the waterslide to hear sounds coming from either bank of the river: yowls and wails, apelike gibberings, human screams of agony. Off to the left they caught the racket of things crashing through undergrowth, splashings, then a string of oaths cut off by a ripping noise, which was in turn followed by a horrible liquid sucking.

"Still looking forward to those other thrills?" Tomokato asked Effluvia.

She made no reply.

Carried on the current, the boat drifted slowly toward the Lost Sea of Borus.

"I think we'd better drop anchor," Tomokato said, and pitched it over the side. "No point going any farther till daylight."

"Do you think we're safe here?" Effluvia asked.

"Yes. I think the whole point of that waterslide is to sink those flimsy paper boats so people have to swim ashore. And be killed by whatever those things are in the woods. If the things could swim, there'd be no need for all that."

"But why would the Pterns want to do such a thing to people?" Effluvia demanded, all her religious assumptions horribly challenged.

"To make sure no one ever returns and tells all Bazoom that the pilgrims don't get their money's worth."

"That's insane," Effluvia said. "It can't be true."

"Listen, Effluvia," Tomokato said grimly, "some people actually give Jerry Lewis medals for the kind of movies he makes. If that's true, anything can be true. Try to get some sleep."

Hours later, Tomokato woke Effluvia to spell him at the watch, then drifted off to sleep himself.

The rattle of machine-gun fire woke him. If his ears served him right, the weapon that had spoken was an Ingram Mac 11 Tiny Tim. Roars and howls came from things on the right-hand bank; then more gunfire and splashing.

He looked over at Effluvia. She had fallen asleep again. He nudged her awake, shifting his gaze back to starboard.

"Is it soup yet?" she asked drowsily.

"Shhh!" he hissed. Something was swimming toward the boat. Mars's second moon had risen; there was just enough light for him to see what appeared to be a man coming through the water, something small and alive clinging to his shoulders.

Suddenly the man stopped dead. "Damn!" Tomokato heard him whisper. "It's a Ptern-boat!"

"Are you pilgrims?" Tomokato called.

There was a moment's hesitation.

"No, Pterns!" Then, in a whisper, the man said to the thing on his back: "Can you get a shot at him?" Apparently the fellow had no idea how much sharper Tomokato's feline hearing was than a man's.

"Wait!" Tomokato cried. "We're not priests. And neither are you, I gather. Come on aboard."

The man started forward again, cautiously, getting near enough to satisfy himself that Tomokato and Effluvia were not Pterns. Then, with Tomokato's aid, he pulled himself up over the gunwale, the little fellow on his back sliding off beside him. With a start Tomokato realized that the small figure was actually a gun-toting kitten. Looking closer, he got an even bigger shock.

"Uncle-*san*?" Shiro cried, peering back at him wide-eyed. "I *thought* I recognized your voice."

Tomokato was absolutely speechless.

"Ptin Kan," Shiro said to his companion, "this is my Uncle Tomokato!"

"Ptin Kan?" cried Effluvia, leaping to her feet.

"Effluvia?" Ptin Kan asked, voice full of amazement.

She rushed over to him, and he threw his arms about her; for the next minute and a half Shiro and Tomokato were treated to a series of passionate plumber's-helper-type smackings. Then Ptin Kan straightened and freed himself from Effluvia's arms.

"Strumpet!" he said haughtily. "I haven't forgotten how you betrayed me!"

"Oh, Ptin Kan!" Effluvia said. "I didn't betray you. How many times must I tell you—"

"That it was the Pthote-Egg Bunny that left the little bastards in your room? Do you think I'm a complete fool?"

A furious argument ensued. Tomokato took Shiro aside.

"When are you going to stop following me?" he asked.

"I *didn't* follow you this time, Uncle. I'm here with the family. We're vacationing. There's this big resort for non-Bazoomians up along the seashore."

"So why aren't you with your parents?"

"Well, that's kind of a long story. . . ."

"Tell me."

"Okay. It's like this. We kept seeing people getting killed by monsters outside the resort. The Pterns who run the place told us that it was all just fake, robots acting it out, like those audio-animatronic figures they have at Disney World. But Dad began to suspect that wasn't what was happening at all, and I began to think a full investigation was needed; so when I saw Ptin Kan here being chased down by a pack of Carrot-Men and Great White Chimps, I snuck over the wall and went to help him. It was just great, Uncle; I got to try out my new gun . . ." Shiro waved the Mac 11. "But boy, did we get lost in the woods."

"I can imagine," Tomokato said. "But why did your father stay on at this resort if such atrocities were happening outside? It doesn't sound very relaxing to me."

"It wasn't his cup of tea, either," Shiro answered. "Not even before he began to suspect—which was kind of strange, if you ask me. It's one thing if innocent people are being killed. But if it's just robot-gush splattering all over the place, that's pretty neat."

Tomokato mulled this over. "But Ptin Kan came here quite a while ago. How did he survive among the monsters so long?"

"He told me the Pterns sometimes pick pilgrims out to be slaves. He escaped from their caves in the mountains—only to find himself here in Paradise." Shiro paused. "Now, Uncle-*san*: what are *you* doing here? Tracking down Zad Fnark?"

"Yes. How did you know?"

"Rona Barrett's column. I don't know why

pthotes."

Tomokato decided not to carry the conversation any further.

When the sun rose they proceeded downriver toward the Lost Sea of Borus. The sea was not far, only two hundred yards or so from the spot where Tomokato had anchored the boat. But having spotted the craft from the riverbanks, the Carrot-Men and Great White Chimps were preparing a reception.

Not far upstream from where the river reached the sea, two huge trees, hundreds of feet tall, stood on either bank. So many Carrot-Men and chimps were swarming out onto their branches that the heavily laden boughs drooped a scant thirty feet above the water.

"They're going to try and jump down into the boat," Ptin Kan announced grimly.

"I'll take care of 'em!" Shiro said, sliding a fresh clip into his Tiny Tim and yanking back the bolt.

"You know, Shiro," Tomokato said before Shiro could start firing, "you really should get a silencer for that."

"But why, Uncle-*san*? I like the noise."

"So you have something to hang onto, control the gun with. That's the trouble with those tiny little machine-pistols. Fantastic rate of fire, but no control—"

Shiro's first burst cut in—the whole magazine gone in an instant. Shredded leaves and wood flew from the drooping boughs ahead, and eighteen or so Carrot-Men and chimps fell screaming toward the Bliss, clutching at their bloody bullet-torn bodies. Shiro looked at his uncle, a hint of smugness on his young face.

"Us little guys are very good with little guns," he said, reloading. By the time he was done with the next two clips, the boughs were hanging a good deal higher above the water. But he was completely out of ammo.

"Your turn now, Uncle," the kitten said.

Tomokato stood, unsheathing his sword as the remaining monsters readied themselves to jump. Ptin Kan rose also, freeing his own blade. But Tomokato wondered if they would even get a chance to use the weapons; would the boat simply be capsized when the creatures leaped down into it?

"First Squad, now!" cried one of the chimps in guttural Bazoomian as the boat passed be-

you adults read trash like that, but I guess she was right about you. Will you take me with you?"

"No. I'm going to drop you off with your parents," Tomokato answered. "Will the Pterns let you back into the resort?"

"I don't know," Shiro replied. "They might not be too pleased that I was out snooping around and rescuing people. I think you'd really better take me with you."

"Out of the question," Tomokato said. "Your parents must be sick with worry."

"Oh, I don't think so. I disappear all the time."

Tomokato looked over toward Effluvia and Ptin Kan. The couple had lapsed into sullen silence and sat facing away from each other.

"I wish I was dead," Effluvia muttered, sobbing.

"I wish you were, too," snapped Ptin Kan.

"That's no way to talk to a woman who's gone through so much to reach your side," Tomokato said.

"Maybe not," the Bazoomian answered. "But it's a good way to talk to one who sleeps with

neath the boughs. A fourth of the remaining monsters leaped from their perches.

Tomokato reached back and goosed a little more speed from the outboard motor. All of the creatures landed some distance astern.

"Second Squad, now!" the leader-chimp cried. But the boat was even farther downstream, and Squad Two also went straight into the drink.

"Squad Three!" bellowed the chimp, determined to see it through. "Squad Four!" Into the river they plunged bravely, like Fenimore Cooper Indians. And with a last salute to no one in particular, the leader-chimp followed them into their watery grave.

"Let that be a lesson to you, Shiro," Tomokato told his nephew. And Shiro remembered it until he was a very old kitten indeed.

The boat passed out into the sea, Tomokato steering to starboard.

"Just keep following the shoreline," Shiro said.

Tomokato looked off to the southwest. A mountainous island loomed up out of the water, many miles away.

"That's Ptern Headquarters out there," said Ptin Kan. "The Isle of Mrs. Blissus."

"Does Mrs. Blissus actually exist?" Tomokato asked.

"I don't know," Ptin Kan answered. "I've never been to the island. But my Ptern masters seemed to assume she was real."

"They might have just been trying to fool you."

"What would they care? I'd already seen what a sham the rest of the religion was."

"We're all going to burn in Hell," Effluvia said gloomily. "They're going to bury us in flaming mausoleums, head down. That's what they do to heretics."

"I thought Dante just made that idea up for *The Inferno*," Shiro said.

"No," Effluvia said. "He picked up the idea here on Bazoom. Look."

She pointed. Sliding along in a gondola off to port were Dante and Virgil, Dante scribbling away furiously in a note pad, Virgil poling.

"How come I always have to pole?" Virgil grumbled.

"Because I've still got to finish the *Commedia*, and you've been dead for thirteen hundred years," Dante snapped back. "Besides, you're

lucky I let you out of Hell at all."

Suddenly they seemed to notice Tomokato's boat.

"Tomokato!" Virgil cried.

"Have we met?" Tomokato asked.

"Not yet. But I've got the Second Sight of the Damned, or the Virtuous Pagans, or whatever category this character here"—Virgil jerked a thumb toward Dante—"dropped me into. Look me up when you get to Hell. Best damn guide you ever heard of. Only safari I ever got into hot water was Gertrude Stein's. Had to leave her in the Bolgia for the Repetitious."

"So I'm going to wind up in Hell, am I?"

"Only on a business trip. Be seeing you."

The gondola dwindled astern as Tomokato steered round a densely-forested point.

"There's the resort," Shiro announced.

At first, all Tomokato could see of it was a massive wall, with the very tops of Earth-style hotels rising into view above it; designed no doubt to insulate the vacationers from the monster-infested wilds that surrounded the area, the barrier ran well out into the sea. Bird-hatted figures moved along the battlements. They soon spotted the boat and collected into several groups, unslinging radium-rifles, pointing.

"Will they shoot?" Tomokato asked Shiro and Ptin Kan.

"Not at a Ptern craft," Shiro said. "They probably think you and I just rented it for the day. But I bet they won't let Effluvia and Ptin Kan through."

"We'll see about that," Tomokato said, and swung out to starboard, rounding the wall. Stretching a half mile and more along a glorious length of white-sanded beach, the resort was an awesome sight, like several blocks of the Strip from Las Vegas transplanted next to a Bazoomian boardwalk.

"Awesome sight, isn't it?" Ptin Kan said. "It's several blocks of the Strip from Las Vegas transplanted next to a Bazoomian boardwalk. The Pterns picked it up cheap after Atlantic City shut Vegas down for good."

Tomokato eased in toward the beach, past a titanic and vulgar statue of Borus flexing his pecs and expanding his chest and looking admiringly at himself in a mirror. But as the craft neared the surf, two fliers came up from behind, skimming along on either side of it, hulls barely touching the water.

"Halt, please," called a Ptern from the one to port.

Tomokato slipped the motor into neutral.

"We'd like to board you," the Ptern cried.

"What for?" Tomokato asked.

"We'd like to check your ID. We were told to watch out for strangely-dressed Earth creatures coming in from the direction of the Bliss."

Tomokato nodded. "By Zad Fnark, right?"

"Right," the Ptern said.

"Well, you found me. You can leave now."

"All right," said the Ptern, and signaled to the other flier. As Tomokato started his engine back up, the two fliers turned back out to sea—then stopped dead. But by the time they caught up to Tomokato, his craft was beached, and he and his party were heading up over the sand, threading their way among sunbathing Earthlings. The fliers floated after them.

"Sir," called the Ptern who had talked to Tomokato, "oh, sir."

Tomokato and his group halted, looking back. "What is it now?" the cat asked.

"You can't bring those er—robots with you," the Ptern said.

"You mean these two?" Tomokato asked, indicating Effluvia and Ptin Kan. "They *do* look amazingly like those robots out in the woods, don't they? But it just so happens they're real people."

"But, sir, I can't . . ." Looking around him, suddenly aware of how many of the tourists were listening to all of this, the Ptern shut up. It just wouldn't do for the guests to find out what was really going on outside the walls.

Tomokato and company headed forward once more, the fliers still following. The cat picked out famous people among the sunbathers: Woodrow Wilson, Mike Douglas, Kenneth Clark kicking sand in Ernest Hemingway's face; off to the right, under a very gaudy beach umbrella, Margaret Thatcher was talking to Douglas MacArthur. Spotting Tomokato, Thatcher waved. Tomokato had met her once when Nobunaga had gone to England to attend an economic summit. The cat and the Iron Lady had discussed *Eight Is Enough* at a banquet.

"Can you believe it?" she cried. "Doug here can't stand Dick Van Patten either!"

MacArthur waved too.

A short distance ahead, Tomokato saw four kittens emerge from behind an umbrella, inflatable swimming-rings around their stomachs; momentarily a handsome fortyish female cat in a

beach kimono, hair let down around her shoulders, came out behind them.

"You're sure you don't want to come in with us, Mama-*san*?" cried one of the kittens, over his shoulder.

"I'll just watch, Huki," she replied. "Make sure you don't get into troub—*Tomokato!*"

The kittens all stopped in their tracks. "Uncle-*san!*" cried Huki, Duki, Luki, and Agamemnon, bowing.

Tomokato bowed in turn. "I have something of yours, Hanako," he said, and pulled Shiro out in front of him.

"Shiro," said Hanako, without the least trace of anger, "did you have a good time in the woods?"

"Sure did, Mama-*san*," said Shiro. "But how did you know where I was?"

Shimura limped into view from around the umbrella. "Some of the guards spotted you lowering yourself down on the bedsheets," he said. "Good to see you again, Tomokato." He bowed.

But Tomokato was flabbergasted by the way they had apparently taken Shiro's absence. "Aren't you upset with him?" he demanded.

Shimura shrugged. "He disappears all the time."

"Excuse me," called the Ptern who had talked to Tomokato. Tomokato turned to face the hovering fliers once more.

"Yes?" he asked.

"I think you'd better accompany us to the security office, sir," the Ptern said. "You and those robots."

"That's all right," Shimura cried to the Ptern as the fliers started to land. "They're all with me."

The Ptern looked exasperated and leaned over to one of his colleagues to accept a few whispered words of advice.

"Very well," he said, straightening. "But I'll have to check this with my superiors."

"You do that," said Shimura.

"Do you mind if I leave a flier here? I'd like to have somebody watching you."

"By all means," Tomokato said. "If we have to make a quick break, a flier might come in very handy."

"Well, I'm glad I can be of some assistance, sir," said the Ptern. His ship rose into the air and headed off toward the Stardust.

"After Zad Fnark, aren't you?" Shimura asked Tomokato.

Tomokato nodded.

"Think you might want some help?"

"You?"

"And the rest of the family. If you'll have us along."

"I'd be delighted," Tomokato said.

"Uncle-*san!*" Shiro cried. "You don't need all of them. Just me."

"What?"

Shiro motioned Tomokato down toward him. "I don't think they'll be worth anything to us," he whispered conspiratorially. "All my brothers ever think about is becoming paramedics. They'd much rather fix people than carve them up. My mother's just a *girl,* of course"—Shiro pronounced *girl* with the purest cootie-horror imaginable—"and as for Dad, he may have been something once, but he's over the hill now. He can hardly walk, and—"

All at once Shiro stopped, noticing the wrath in Tomokato's eyes.

"Well, it's the truth, isn't it?" the kitten asked, plucking up his nerve.

Tomokato looked at Shimura. "Did you hear any of that?" he asked.

Shimura just laughed. "Was he selling his father short again?"

"That child!" Hanako said. "Shimura, you should—"

Shimura folded his arms on his chest. "If he hasn't learned after all the spankings I've given him already, one more won't do any good. I think he'll just have to learn his lesson some other way." He winked at Tomokato.

Out of the corner of his eye, Tomokato noticed a blot of shadow moving over the beach off to his left; casting it was a large, ornate flier cruising toward the sea. He guessed the craft had come from one of the rooftop landing-pads on the hotels. Leaning on the stern rail, talking to the Pterns on either side of him, a martini in his hand, was Zad Fnark. So engrossed in his conversation was the assassin that he did not seem to notice Tomokato. What *was* this man's connection to the Pterns?

"Zad Fnark," Tomokato said to Shimura, pointing. "Can you come with me now?"

Shimura looked at the Ptern craft that had been left behind to guard them. "In that flier, I

suppose?"

"How else?" Tomokato asked.

"Sure we can," Shimura said. "As it just so happens, we brought all our luggage to the beach today."

"What a stroke of luck," Tomokato said. "Go get it."

Accelerating rapidly, Zad Fnark's flier sped out over the Lost Sea of Borus, heading straight for the Isle of Mrs. Blissus.

"You know how to fly one of those things?" Tomokato asked Ptin Kan.

Ptin Kan nodded.

"Good," Tomokato said. "We won't need to capture any Pterns then."

"But what if I don't want to come with you?" Ptin Kan asked.

"Only wackos would want to trespass on the Isle of Mrs. Blissus!" Effluvia added.

"It's not as if you two can just stay here without us," Tomokato said. "We're your best hope to get out of this valley."

Shimura and his family reappeared from behind their umbrella, each carrying a suitcase. All had changed out of their beach togs and

73

back into everyday sixteenth-century Japanese duds.

"You should listen to Tomokato, my dear," Hanako told Effluvia.

"Well, at least let's leave the floozy here!" said Ptin Kan angrily, nodding Effluvia's way. "You don't need her to work the flier, Tomokato!"

"I think you should just thank your Bazoomian gods that *you* never woke up with a clutch of pthote-eggs in *your* bedroom, Ptin Kan," Tomokato replied.

"You mean you believe her about the bunny?" Ptin Kan demanded.

"I didn't say that," Tomokato replied. "But are you perfect? Do you have the right to judge her? Perhaps you should show a little compassion."

As if stung by Tomokato's words, Ptin Kan was silent for a few moments, brows knit.

"I'm afraid not," he said at last. "My moral imperfections have nothing whatsoever to do with hers. Even if I *was* as reprehensible as she is, that would merely drive me to have the same kind of contempt for myself that I now have for her. But I'm not as reprehensible in any case. So where's your argument? Are you seriously suggesting that only moral paragons are fit to judge others? If so, temporal justice is an absurdity, an impossibility. And where does that leave you and your quest for retribution, Mr. Samurai Cat?"

"Good answer," said Shimura.

"All right," Tomokato said, simmering. "Let's board that flier."

Leading the troop, he went over to the craft.

"Yes?" asked the Ptern commander.

"We need your ship now," Tomokato said.

"I don't know about this . . ."

"Did you see that big flier that just passed? There's a man on it I have to kill, and we really must have your flier to follow him."

The Ptern winced. "I'll get in trouble. . . ."

"No you won't," Tomokato assured him.

"All right, if you say so. But I'm telling you, if my superiors get mad about this, I'm going to get even madder at you."

"I accept all responsibility."

"Okay. Come on, men. Let's get off.

The Ptern and his crew climbed over the side. Tomokato and crew climbed aboard. Ptin Kan went up on the bridge.

"It'll be a few seconds," he announced, looking over the controls. "I'm not quite familiar with this sort of setup."

"Don't worry," Tomokato said. "I think we'll be all right. . . ."

"Don't let them have your flier, you fools!" a voice bellowed.

Tomokato whirled to see the craft that had flown off toward the Stardust returning, its commander hopping mad in the bow.

"Don't listen to him," Tomokato told the Pterns. They stood there numbly for an instant, badly confused. Then one snarled:

"What the hey . . ."

Tomokato drew his sword as the Pterns came pelting back. The priests had rifles but made no effort to use them; having drawn his steel before they could unsling their guns, Tomokato had defined the limits of combat, according to Martian chivalry. He did not think Martian chivalry made much sense, but he was happy to take advantage of it.

A Ptern hurdled the rail in front of him, brandishing a blade. Tomokato's sword caught him in midair, knocking him back over the side playing yo-ho-ho with his slithering guts.

Two more vaulted the barrier, dashing in from right and left. Tomokato stepped toward one and sliced him into unheavenly hash; then the cat pivoted to meet the other, ducking a blow and taking the poor jerk to pieces with a series of blows called the Tokyo Tenderizer.

The flier lurched and began to rise. Perched on a rail, a Ptern lost his footing and fell back to the beach. Effluvia was strangling another with her impossibly long Frazettaesque hair. Beyond her, two more were arguing loudly over the privilege of killing Shiro, who had his back to the superstructure and stood snarling up at them, swinging his empty Tiny Tim.

Sitting it all out, Shimura, Hanako, and Shiro's brothers were taking it all in from the bridge.

"So far, so good, Tomokato," Shimura cried. "But you'd better watch out for that other flier!"

Tomokato turned. The craft was making straight for them, deck swarming with Pterns, smoke streaming for its hibachis.

But before it could close the gap, the whole thing went up like the Hindenburg gone cranky. Below, sun-worshippers scattered to get away from the falling debris and bits of bodies.

"Nice shooting, Woody!" Tomokato heard

Maggie Thatcher cry, and looked over at Woodrow Wilson. Looking very proud on his Pac-Man beach blanket, the Prez cast his smoking Stinger-launcher aside.

"Okay, Tomokato!" yelled Shimura. "Now save that brat kid of mine!"

Tomokato leaped past Effluvia, who was still in the process of murdering her Ptern. "Oh well, after you, Alphonse," said one of the two facing Shiro, and his companion raised his blade to strike.

Tomokato got there first. Large parts of their bodies edited into oblivion, the Pterns fell dead.

"That's the last of 'em!" Shimura cried.

Tomokato looked round to see Effluvia's priest lying dead at her feet. The flier sped seaward to the sound of loud applause from the tourists below.

But it wasn't over yet. A whole fleet of Ptern fliers rose from the hotel rooftops and swept out over the beach.

"More trouble!" Tomokato cried.

Yet hardly were the words out of his mouth when hundreds of Stinger-launchers appeared on the shoulders of the tourists, whipped out from under blankets and towels, or from inside coolers; if a single sunbather back there didn't have one, Tomokato was greatly mistaken. And every one of the tubes was pointed at the Ptern fleet.

Very quickly, the Pterns wheeled round and landed back atop the hotels.

"Ah," said Hanako. "That was nice, wasn't it?"

Tomokato went up on the bridge. "Any chance we can catch Zad Fnark?" he asked Ptin Kan.

"Not in this ship," the Bazoomian replied. "That was a top-of-the-line Ptern shuttle he was on."

"What keeps this thing in the air?" Tomokato asked. "I know the propellers drive it, but what provides the flotation?"

"All Bazoomian technology is based on the Nine Rays," Ptin Kan replied. "Tanks filled with the Eighth, or Aldo, Ray, are located in the hull. They create an antigravity field."

"I see," Tomokato said. "Do you have any

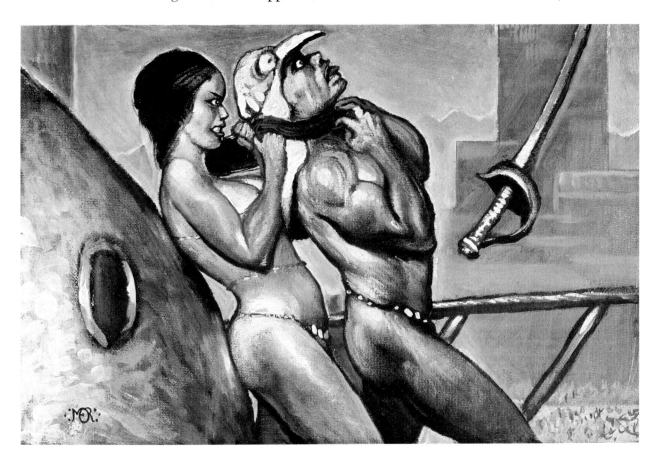

Tomokato asked him. "I want to meet Zad Fnark—face to face."

Before the Ptern could answer, Shimura came up beside his brother.

"We could pretend to be his prisoners," Shimura said. "With Agamemnon holding that string, he'd have to cooperate. How we'd locate Zad Fnark is another matter, of course."

"I've got a hunch we'd be taken to him in any case," Tomokato said. "He seems to wield considerable authority among the Pterns, though I haven't guessed why."

The Ptern on the deck below gave him a strange look at that point, then quickly turned his head.

"What does Zad Fnark have to do with your priesthood?" Tomokato asked.

"You'll find out soon enough," the Ptern replied.

"You want us to make him talk?" Agamemnon asked thuggishly, tightening his grip on the string. "We can pop 'im one section at a time. . . ."

"Let him be," Tomokato said, repulsed by the thought of torture. "Haven't you little paramedics ever heard of the Hippocratic Oath?"

"Sure we have, Uncle-*san*," said Duki. "We'd just get a big kick out of putting him back together again."

Tomokato sighed. Their interests were channeled in a different direction, but perhaps they were not so different from Shiro after all.

"I thought of a splendid poem while watching you fight the Pterns," Shimura said. "You really inspired me."

Tomokato smiled. "I'm delighted."

Shimura went on: "It's kind of an unauthorized addition to *Old Possum's*, called 'Maniacal Cats.' "

"Would you recite it for me?"

"Not yet. Have to polish it a bit."

"Later, then," Tomokato said, and went down from the bridge. Seated on deck chairs, Effluvia and Hanako were talking earnestly.

"There, there," he heard Hanako saying. "Certainly I believe you."

Tomokato looked around for Shiro, heard someone rummaging around inside the cabin, and went through the hatch, arriving just in time to see Shiro finding two Mac 11 clips in a drawer beneath a radium-rifle rack. But Shiro did not appear to be delighted by his discovery; hardly paying any attention to his uncle at all,

idea of how we can penetrate Ptern Headquarters?"

"Maybe we can help there, Uncle-*san!*" cried Luki. The kitten was down beside the superstructure with Huki, Duki, and Agamemnon, all of them paramedicking mightily away at one of the Pterns Tomokato had dismembered, reaching into little black bags for one surgical instrument after another; where they had gotten the whole blood in those transfusion bottles, Tomokato couldn't possibly guess.

"What do you have in mind, Luki?" he asked.

"This guy might be able to give us the information," Luki replied.

"You mean that corpse?"

"I meant just what I said, Uncle-*san*," Luki answered, and snapped a vial of smelling salts under the Ptern's nose. The Ptern winced and sat up, very much alive.

"No funny business now," said Agamemnon, holding a length of stitching attached to a sewn-up wound in the Ptern's side. "One good tug on this, and you're back in pieces."

The Ptern gulped.

"How can we get inside your headquarters?"

he sat on the floor and sullenly reloaded his gun, shoving the other magazine into his kimono.

"What's the matter, Shiro?" Tomokato asked, sitting next to him.

"I'm so embarrassed," Shiro said.

"By what?"

"Dad," the kitten replied.

"Shiro," Tomokato said sternly, "it's your duty to respect your father."

"He didn't even try to help you during the fight," Shiro answered. "He's not just a cripple. He's a coward, too."

"You know, Shiro," Tomokato said, barely restraining his temper, "if it wasn't for the fact that your father doesn't think it would do any good, I'd spank you myself. And let me tell you this: Your father's no coward. He was simply composing a poem, that's all."

"A poem," Shiro sneered.

Tomokato stood up in disgust. "I don't know what to do with you," he said, and strode from the cabin.

"Having a serious interlude, Tomokato?" Hanako asked from her deck chair.

Tomokato nodded grimly.

On swept the flier toward the Isle of Mrs. Blissus. The distance narrowed swiftly. Vast complexes of citadels and palaces stood out among the island's well-forested slopes. The sheer opulence of the structures was beyond anything Tomokato had ever seen; but given the loot the Pterns had been picking up tax-free for the last five thousand years, it came as no surprise.

There were several large landing fields. The captive Ptern refused to tell which one serviced Ptern Headquarters—until Tomokato and Shimura agreed to let Agamemnon bluff him with torture threats. The field was located in the center of the island, beside a huge domed building with the look of some kind of temple.

Learning the flier could land on automatic, Tomokato had everyone gather in the cabin before the craft descended. As it came down, he scanned the field outside, noticing that the flier Zad Fnark had taken was resting on the ground nearby.

"Will Zad Fnark be in the temple?" he asked the prisoner.

"I expect so," the man replied.

Tomokato smiled mirthlessly. "Agamemnon," he said, "stay close to this Ptern here. If he makes the slightest wrong move, pull the string."

"Got it, Uncle-*san*," said Agamemnon.

"As for you," Tomokato said, indicating the Ptern, "take this." He handed him an unloaded radium-rifle. "Pretend to cover us with it. I'll whisper what I want you to say when we reach those guards by the entrance. As for the rest of you, remember that you're supposed to be prisoners."

"What about our swords?" Ptin Kan asked Tomokato. "Won't the guards notice them?"

Tomokato thought a bit. "You grab Luki, and I'll grab Duki. We'll hold them in front of our scabbards."

Ptin Kan snapped his fingers. "By the gods, I wish I could come up with ideas like that." He picked Duki up, tried to position him satisfactorily. "He's too small. He doesn't cover the whole scabbard."

"You worry too much," Duki said. "If this doesn't work, Uncle-*san* will just kill everyone in sight." The kitten shifted uncomfortably in the Bazoomian's grip. "You've got very sweaty palms, do you know that?"

"Let's be off," Tomokato said. Leaving the cabin, they lowered the gangway and headed

over to the temple steps. With his limp, Shimura had some difficulty negotiating the steps.

Tomokato saw Shiro glancing over at his father, shaking his head.

"I wish *you* were my dad, Uncle-*san,*" the kitten announced.

"If you ever say such a thing again," Tomokato snarled, "I *will* spank you, with your father's permission or not."

"Ah, he's such a wimp, he'd let you do whatever you wanted to."

"That does it," Tomokato said, almost going after him then and there—before realizing he would have to drop Luki and uncover his scabbard.

"I didn't think you'd do it," Shiro said. "You know I'm right."

Tomokato just growled. The group continued upward.

"Halt!" cried the guards at the door.

"Say: Prisoners for Zad Fnark!" whispered Tomokato to the Ptern behind him.

The Ptern shouted it to the guards.

"Zad Fnark, eh?" one of them asked suspiciously. He pointed to Shiro. "Is that a gun that 'prisoner' is holding?"

Immediately realizing the man was referring to his Tiny Tim, which was hanging in front of him on its strap, Shiro grabbed Huki, holding him in front of the gun.

"What are you talking about?" Shiro asked. "It must be the wind!"

"Too small to be a real gun, Smitty," said the other guard to his companion.

"Can't let these bozos through, though," said Smitty, and casually pressed a button on the pillar beside him.

Instantly the steps beneath Tomokato's group flattened out, becoming a ramp that swung downward on squealing hinges, pitching the whole crowd into a steep dark chute. As they plunged farther and farther down the incline, Tomokato felt some kind of vapor sweep his face, and caught a musty, drowsy scent that was almost, but not quite, the olfactory equivalent of a Perry Como Christmas Special. Then consciousness left him.

When he woke, he was in a great gold-decked hall, lying on the floor. In front of him was an empty throne mounted on a dais. Armed Pterns guarded all doorways. Off to one side were the other members of his party; most of them had regained consciousness, or were in the process of doing so. And like him, they had their paws (or hands) tied behind their backs.

He tried to get up just as a richly-dressed Ptern in a spectacular bird-hat that covered his whole head emerged from an opening beside the throne, followed by two guards.

"Grovel, Earth-creature!" snarled a voice behind Tomokato, and a series of blows forced him back down. "Grovel before Psingapore Psling, High Priest of Mrs. Blissus, Goddess of Immortality!"

"Bring him and the girl forward," said Psingapore Psling, voice muffled inside his headdress. Tomokato and Effluvia were dragged up onto the dais.

"Ah, Effluvia," said the High Priest. "So lovely. You shall be my concubine."

"How do you know my name?" Effluvia demanded.

"I peeked at your dog tags."

"My dog tags!" Effluvia cried. "Have you no shame? Have you no respect for my privacy?" She paused. "Wait a minute. I don't even have dog tags."

Psingapore Psling laughed evilly. "I lied. Actually, I had your name from Zad Fnark. He thought you'd please me. And indeed you will. By Mrs. Blissus, you're stacked!" A slurping noise echoed hollowly within the bird-head.

"And as for you," he said, turning to Tomokato, "I understand you've caused a great deal of trouble in our realm. And all of it just to kill one man."

"Give me Zad Fnark," Tomokato said.

Psingapore Psling laughed again. "Are you really in any position to make such a demand?"

"Give me Zad Fnark now, and loose my bonds," Tomokato said.

"I'd do it if I were you," Effluvia advised the Ptern. "You don't know what he's capable of."

"Oh, I've got a pretty fair idea," said the High Priest.

"Then spare yourself," Tomokato said. "Give me what I want. I won't ask again."

"Very well," said Psingapore Psling, and removed his headdress.

Tomokato's eyes widened. "Zad Fnark!" he gritted.

"I don't go by that name around here," the High Priest said. "That's how the guards at the door knew something was fishy. No Ptern would

ever call me that—but your prisoner did." He raised his hands. "Well, here I am, yours for the taking. But I'm afraid I'll have to disappoint you on the matter of untying your bonds. That would make it so much more risky to do this. . . ." Leaning forward, he poked Tomokato in the eyes with two fingers. "Or this . . ." Curley Howard-style, he flapped his hand under Tomokato's nose, slapping his face upward. "Or this!" With a wild, ear-splitting shriek, he kicked Tomokato powerfully in the mouth, sending a cracked tooth flying.

"Uncle-*san!*" Shiro cried.

"Dog!" cried Shimura at Zad Fnark.

"Cat!" Zad Fnark replied. "What's the matter? Don't you like the Three Stooges?"

"Nobody really got hurt on *The Three Stooges*," Shimura retorted. "Those men were trained comedians. The violence looked real, but they were just faking it. You should never try that

sort of thing by yourself!"

"Spoken like a true petit bourgeois! I suppose if I was going to pound myself in the face with an axe, you'd try to talk me out of that, too."

"Of course."

Zad Fnark snapped his fingers at one of his men. "Quick, fetch me an axe!"

The man hurried off, returning moments later with a mean-looking double-bladed item.

"Now just watch me!" crowed Zad Fnark to Shimura, taking the weapon and poising it before his face with both hands.

"Hold, High Priest!" came an old woman's voice. Spitting blood, Tomokato saw an incredibly ancient female appear through the doorway beside the throne, accompanied by a pair of voluptuous serving-maids, who, for lack of flowers (flowers were very scarce on Bazoom), were sprinkling gaily-colored ceremonial moss on her

head and shoulders.

"Mrs. Blissus!" said Zad Fnark, and knelt. All the other Pterns knelt, too. With a surprisingly sure tread for one so aged, the goddess proceeded to the throne; even after she sat down, the serving-maids continued raining moss on her.

"Who *are* these two?" Mrs. Blissus asked at last, pointing to the girls, arms crossed over her withered bosom.

"You mean they're not your slaves, O Goddess of Eternal Life?" asked Zad Fnark.

"Hell no," the old woman answered.

Giggling, the two girls ran off.

"Seize them and spank them!" cried Zad Fnark to several of his men. They rushed to do his bidding.

"Now where were we?" Zad Fnark said, once more preparing to axe himself in the face.

"Knock that off, dammit!" shouted Mrs. Blissus.

"If you say so, Your Extreme Leatheryness," he replied, lowering the weapon.

"Who's that?" the goddess asked, indicating Tomokato.

"The Earth-creature that's been trying to kill me. All the rest came with him."

"Why's he trying to kill you?"

"Because I was involved in the murder of his lord."

"I *told* you that hobby of yours was going to get you in trouble! You and your assassinations!"

"Sorry," Zad Fnark said, looking down at his fingernails. "I *have* killed a lot of important people, though."

"Did you see that letter from the Bulgarians? Just came in today?"

"Haven't had time to check the mail. But anyway: what should we do with him?"

"The Earth-creature?" Mrs. Blissus asked. "Can he fight?"

"Like a demon."

"Good. Let's chuck him in the arena."

"I was hoping you'd say that, Your Petrifiedness." Zad Fnark kicked the cat again. "Just kiss your ass goodbye, pussy."

Tomokato glared at him in silent hatred. Zad Fnark signaled. A host of guards hustled Tomokato and his companions from the throne room, in and out of broad corridors decorated with decadent and sleazy bas-reliefs; out of the temple they went and into the coliseumlike structure standing behind it. The guards untied Tomokato's paws just before pushing him down a greased slide into the arena; once they raised the slide out of his reach, they tossed his sword to him, then herded the other members of his group over to an ornate pavilion on the far side of the arena, where Zad Fnark and Mrs. Blissus appeared after a time, having come by another route.

Tomokato eyed the walls. They were too high to bound over, even with his earthly leaping abilities. He saw no means of escape.

There was a twenty-minute wait while the stands filled up and the network people got their act together. Then, when the cameras were ready, and the joint was packed, and everybody had gotten their sodas, and hot dogs cooked in beer, Zad Fnark silenced the throng.

"Today, in full view of his friends and loved ones, this malignant creature"—the High Priest pointed to the cat—"will meet his richly-deserved end as a sacrifice to our beloved goddess, Mrs. Blissus!"

"Yeah!" whooped the crowd. "*Mis-*sus *Blis-*sus! *All Right!*"

"May She, in Her Infinite Wisdom, grant that he gives us a damn fine show!"

"*Mis-*sus *Blis-*sus! *All Right!*" chanted the crowd.

"Let the festivities begin!" cried the High Priest, and sat down on a marble chair beside Mrs. Blissus's throne, pulling Effluvia into his lap. An expectant hush settled over the crowd.

Slowly, directly in front of Tomokato, a section of wall slid upward. Out came two huge Green Meanies, pushed forward into the arena by a moving barrier covered with spikes. Swords flashing in the sun, they stormed toward him; the crowd roared, mad with bloodlust.

Tomokato charged, waiting till the last moment to leap airborne. Sailing between the two creatures, he sheared through one's neck. But before his sword could strike the other, the monster flung his blade up, deflecting the blow.

Landing behind the Green Meanie, Tomokato whirled; the thing pivoted toward him, blade thrusting. Tomokato shattered the weapon with his parry and leaped toward the Meanie's face,

slicing. There was a sound like a cleaver splitting a cantaloupe, a spatter of red, and the top of the creature's head flew off like a beanie in a gale. Tomokato landed atop the corpse as it crumpled to the ground.

Another roar from the crowd, and a roll of many great padded feet; he spun to see a giant war-pthote bearing down on him. Instantly Effluvia's chant sprang into his mind, and he cried:

> "Big old pthotie-poo,
> Don't hurt me.
> Let me—"

But this big old pthotie-poo wasn't buying. Whatever he had done wrong, Tomokato couldn't guess, but he wasn't going to waste time trying to figure it out. The creature pounded close; he dodged aside, then slashed into one of its forelegs. With a bellow, the pthote stumbled forward onto the Green Meanie's corpse and flipped completely over, landing thunderously on its back, legs waving in the air. Leaping between the churning limbs, Tomokato landed on its chest and drove his sword straight downward into its heart. Blood fountained as he withdrew his blade.

Tomokato got down from the pthote's shuddering corpse and strode out into the center of the arena, ignoring the jeers and catcalls from the audience. He was a bit surprised by the lack of respect. He was, at the very least, giving them a damn fine show.

To right and left, two doorways opened. From one poured a horde of Great White Chimps, from the other, a stream of Carrot-Men. Tomokato decided to take the Carrot-Men first; racing to meet their onslaught, he tore into them like a berserk Cuisinart, dicing and shredding and pureeing, scattering the ground with chunks of bodies, sending gouts of V-8 juice splashing through the air.

Before long he was at the wall, and set his back to it to face the onrushing chimps. Straight into his blazing steel they came, and the chimpburger began to fly; for a grisly half minute it was *Bedtime for Bonzo* in spades. Then the last chimp went down, choking on its own blood, gurgling something about Dave Garroway.

Suddenly Tomokato felt the wall behind him sliding upward; in the heat of combat, he had put his back to one of the doorways. Bounding across a waste of dead chimps and Carrot-Men,

he sped back to the middle of the arena, then turned.

His next opponent came slowly toward him. It was a six-legged Blampf, or Giant Bazoomian Lion; well-attuned to feline expressions, Tomokato read a very dispirited mood on the creature's face, and noticed that the Blampf was favoring its left foreleg.

"Oh, my aching paw!" the big cat cried in the Universal Feline Tongue.

"What's the matter?" Tomokato called, in the same language.

"I've got a pthorn in it," the Blampf replied.

"If you'll do me a favor, I'll pull it out for you."

The Blampf's face brightened. "Really?"

"Really."

"Pull it out, pull it out."

To a storm of boos and hisses from the crowd, Tomokato went up to the Blampf and pulled the pthorn out.

"All right now," Tomokato said. "Pretend to come after me, then let me back you over by Mrs. Blissus's pavilion."

"Got it," said the lion, and took a swipe at him. Tomokato leaped back. The Blampf followed but soon retreated before a barrage of strokes that Tomokato pulled at the last moment. This seemed to satisfy the audience at first—by the time they noticed there was no blood, the Blampf was already beneath the pavilion.

And then it was too late.

Tomokato jumped up onto the lion's back; from that extra height, he easily sprang to the top of the wall. Mrs. Blissus's guards gawked— and died.

Tossing Effluvia aside, Zad Fnark put himself between Tomokato and the goddess, reaching for his sword.

Tomokato took his hand off at the wrist.

Screaming, the High Priest raised his bloody stump and tried to squirt the cat in the face with it. Batting it aside with the flat of his blade, Tomokato slashed him across the chest.

"That for Nobunaga!" he cried. "And *this*"— his *katana* whistled down into Zad Fnark's forehead, splitting his skull to the teeth—"for JFK!" Blood cascading over his chin, the Ptern dropped in a heap.

More guards were surging in toward the pavilion. Mrs. Blissus made a dash for the near-

est exit—only to have Effluvia grab her by the hair and fling her down, pointing a dead Ptern's sword at her throat.

"One step closer, and she buys the farm!" Effluvia cried to the onrushing guards.

They stopped dead in their tracks.

"Oh, very good, Effluvia!" cried Hanako from off to the side, clapping her paws.

"Tell your men to cut my companions' bonds," Tomokato snarled to Mrs. Blissus.

She did so. They swiftly obeyed her.

"Arm yourselves," said Tomokato to his party. Huki, Duki, Luki, and Agamemnon picked up shortswords from the scattered corpses; Ptin Kan took a long blade, looking over at Effluvia all the while, very thoughtfully.

"That's quite a girl you've got there," Hanako told him. "And she's not lying about the bunny, either. I can tell about things like that."

Effluvia looked at Ptin Kan. He turned away.

Tomokato eyed Hanako and Shimura. "No swords for you?"

Shimura smiled. "No need. They never searched us, you know."

Tomokato nodded.

Shiro came up holding his Tiny Tim. One of the guards had had it.

"Where to now, Uncle-*san*?" he asked.

"The landing field," Tomokato said.

Effluvia motioned Mrs. Blissus to her feet.

"Keep a sharp eye on the goddess there," Tomokato cautioned. "Shiro, back Effluvia up."

Making their way from the arena, followed by a great crowd of angry Pterns, they went round the temple to the fliers. Ptin Kan selected the fastest-looking one he could find, and shortly they were airborne.

But the flier did not prove as fast as Ptin Kan had hoped. And as they swept over the island's slopes and out toward the Lost Sea of Borus, scores of Ptern craft appeared astern.

"Don't worry," Tomokato said, watching them. "They won't do anything as long as we've got Mrs. Blissus."

Ptin Kan steered southeast toward the Hartz Mountains, on a course that would give the earthling resort a wide berth. Mile by mile, the Ptern fleet gained behind. Soon Tomokato could

clearly see the faces of the priests on the foremost fliers.

A grunt behind him; he looked back. To his horror, he saw Mrs. Blissus standing over the inert form of Effluvia. Shiro trained his Mac 11 on the goddess and pulled the trigger—but he had forgotten to yank back the bolt.

Mrs. Blissus snatched the gun from his paws, cackling.

Tomokato bounded past his nephew, sword sweeping; the old woman retreated with characteristically ungeriatric speed, priming the gun—and tripped. The fall was the only thing that saved her from the slash. Landing flat on her back, gasping, she fired a short, wild burst.

Tomokato took two bullets through the breastplate.

Hardly feeling the impacts, he struck at her again; but the sword flew from his nerveless paws, and he dropped beside her, blackness billowing into his mind.

"Uncle!" Shiro wailed. "Uncle!"

"Get back with the others," growled Mrs. Blissus, rising, clutching the Mac 11.

Shiro backed toward his parents.

"You on the bridge!" the goddess cried to Ptin Kan. "Get down here!"

Ptin Kan complied, leaving the flier to drift.

"Come on, boys!" Mrs. Blissus shouted, beckoning to her warriors astern. "Come and get 'em! It's torture time!"

"Wrong," said Hanako demurely.

"Who says so?" Mrs. Blissus grated, turning the gun toward her.

"Two little friends of mine," Hanako replied. "Say hello, bitch."

She jerked her arms up; two Travis Bickle hideout rigs propelled a pair of neat little .22 automatics out of her voluminous sleeves, into her paws. An instant later small round holes started popping open all over Mrs. Blissus's hideous old face, and the goddess went to the deck with both magazines in her brain. Shouts of rage rose from the watching Pterns.

Huki, Duki, Luki, and Agamemnon raced over to tend Tomokato. Ptin Kan rushed to get back to the controls. Shiro gasped at his mother.

"Not bad for a girl, huh?" she asked him. "Over to you, Shimura."

Shimura turned to face the oncoming Ptern fliers. Stunned by the death of their goddess,

the Pterns had not yet unslung their rifles. Shimura grinned fiercely, whipping out two ivory-handled Colt .45 automatics. Now the limits of combat were set; since the priests had no handguns, they had to settle for the next level down—hundreds of blades flashed from scabbards as the Ptern craft closed in.

"All set, Hanako?" Shimura asked.

"All set," she replied, taking up position behind him.

Shiro ran up beside his father with the Mac 11.

"You won't need that," Shimura said. "Just watch. You might learn something."

The .45's roared, spewing out slugs and spent casings. Splish-splashes of bright scarlet burst from the Pterns on the two foremost craft, and bodies whirled and buckled. Eighteen shots later (Shimura always kept a round in the chamber) their decks were cleared.

Shimura flipped the pistols over his shoulders to Hanako, who deftly snatched them from the air, reloaded them, and thrust them into her sash. Shimura, meanwhile, produced a second brace of Colts and swept two more decks with flying lead; dead and dying Pterns toppled over the railings, plummeted toward the Lost Sea of Borus, trailing blood. Pistols emptied, Shimura tossed the guns back to Hanako, pulled out another brace and another . . .

Shiro stared at him in pop-eyed wonder. Never in his wildest dreams had he guessed that his father was capable of such glorious wholesale slaughter. It was like *The Wild Bunch Goes to Mars*, only with Ben Johnson and Warren Oates and Ernest Borgnine and William Holden compressed into a single figure. And that figure was his own papa!

Finally running out of pistols (his kimono could just hold so many), Shimura signaled Hanako to start tossing him the reloaded ones. Two at a time, they hurtled back into his paws, and the carnage continued unabated, with him flipping her back the empties. The Pterns tried to flank them, to come in from above or up from underneath; no good. Even when Shimura couldn't get a shot at the men on the deck, he blasted the flotation tanks full of holes, and the fliers went down with their Aldo Rays leaking out.

But at last Hanako was out of ammo, and Shimura was running out of reloaded guns. As

his last pistol went dry, the last Ptern flier got close enough for the last surviving warrior aboard to leap the gap. It was the Ptern that Huki, Duki, Luki, and Agamemnon had put back together. Ducking a sweep of the Ptern's sword, Shimura calmly grabbed the string still protruding from the stitching and pulled it. There was a sound like a dozen zippers coming undone at once, and the Ptern fell to pieces like a house of cards.

"Splendid, Father!" Shiro cried. "Just splendid!"

Shimura smiled at him.

"I think you actually missed a shot or two," Hanako told her husband.

Shimura sighed. "Getting old, Hanako," he said ruefully.

Shell-casings rattled on the deck behind them; the whole rear of the flier was two inches deep in expended cartridges from Shimura's guns. Turning, they saw Tomokato coming toward them, looking perfectly fit, accompanied by the paramedic kittens, who appeared very pleased with themselves indeed.

"Your sons certainly know your trade," Tomokato told Shimura and Hanako. Flushing with pride at their children's surgical prowess, they bowed.

"Uncle-*san*!" Shiro cried. "Did you see what my father did?"

"Some of it. Are you more impressed with him now?"

Shiro nodded excitedly. "He's every bit as deadly as you are, Uncle!"

"Yes," Tomokato replied happily.

"What about Effluvia?" Hanako asked Agamemnon. "Did you take a look at her?"

"She was just knocked out," the kitten replied. "No big deal."

"Effluvia!" Hanako called. The Martian woman was already sitting up, but if she heard, she gave no sign of it; she seemed to be staring fixedly at something behind a hibachi.

"Must still be dazed," Hanako said, starting toward her.

"Ptin Kan!" Effluvia shouted, leaping up. "Ptin Kan, come here! Everyone, come and see!"

Ptin Kan descended from the bridge; the others rushed over. Effluvia pointed. And there, in a tidy pile atop a coil of rope, was a clutch of pthote-eggs.

"Merry pthote-eggs to all, and to all a good night!" came a distinctly bunnyish cry. Whirling, they caught a glimpse of an obviously supernatural rabbit in a Santa suit leaping over the side of the flier. Dashing to the rail, they looked down; there was no sign of the bunny below.

But none of them doubted what they had seen.

Ptin Kan and Effluvia rushed into each other's arms and just about sucked each other's faces off.

"Isn't that sweet?" said Hanako as the flier drifted toward the Hartz Mountains.

III. The Empire State Strikes Back

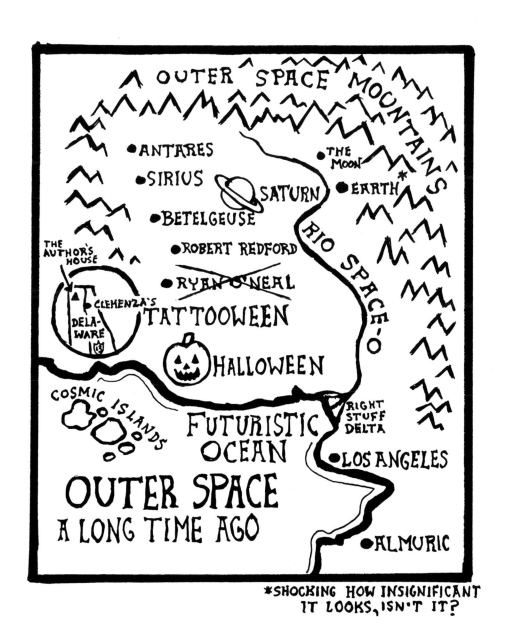

OUTER SPACE MOUNTAINS

• ANTARES

• SIRIUS

SATURN

• BETELGEUSE

• ROBERT REDFORD

• ~~RYAN O'NEAL~~

THE MOON

• EARTH *

RIO SPACE-O

THE AUTHOR'S HOUSE

CLEMENZA'S DELAWARE

TATTOOWEEN

HALLOWEEN

COSMIC ISLANDS

FUTURISTIC OCEAN

RIGHT STUFF DELTA

• LOS ANGELES

OUTER SPACE
A LONG TIME AGO

• ALMURIC

*SHOCKING HOW INSIGNIFICANT
IT LOOKS, ISN'T IT?

The group flew to Lithium, Bazoom's largest city. There Tomokato took his leave of Ptin Kan and Effluvia, saw Shimura's family onto a ship bound for Earth, then took Luftwaffethansa Flight 443 to a galaxy far (but not far far) away, straight into the heart of the dreaded Empire State. This time his prey was Imperial Governor-at-Large Grand Moff Cuomo, and Cuomo's awesome henchman, Darth Shatner; landing on Dykstraflex 5, the Imperial Capital, Tomokato discovered they were off rebel-bashing in the Boonies (the Boonies Star-cluster), and hopped a shuttle for Tattooween, the only planet in that area with a spaceport. . . .

—Cat Out of Hell

Ripped by laser-fire, all four engines out, the Senatorial Ship was overtaken even as she entered the Fosselius System; flagship of the Empire State's fleet, the Empire State Building locked onto the smaller craft with her tractor beams and eased her up into the enormous cargo-bay yawning to receive her in the forty-fifth floor.

Inside the Senatorial Ship, marines scurried to take defensive positions for their final stand, laser-pistols ready. Officers barked orders. Technicians and adorable robots withdrew into the center of the ship.

Three muffled synchronous detonations told of mines blasting the outer airlock hatches in; then came the clang of charges being placed against the inner hatches, and moments later those barriers shattered too. In poured swarms of Imperial SS, blazing away maniacally at their foes. In the great tradition of movie SS everywhere, they could not hit the side of a barn (there were barns at the end of each corridor, and they kept missing them), but they were so heavily armored that they swept effortlessly down the passageways in spite of the intense fire from the marines; grabbing the marines bodily, they pressed their guns right up against their heads,

firing point-blank, managing to kill quite a few of them that way.

When it was over, a huge figure garbed in black appeared in the port hatchway, face concealed behind a black plastic mask that made him look more than a little like Robot Commando. Cape streaming out behind him, he strode massively toward a group of SS Oberlieutenants, who clicked their heels together and saluted.

"My Lord," one said, "we have the Princess." He signaled, and a trooper brought the Princess Pleia Piano forward. She stared defiantly up at the black-clad giant, who folded his arms on his chest and nodded his helmeted head in satisfaction.

"Darth Shatner," the Princess said. "Only you would be so bold, attacking a Senatorial Ship. The media will not sit still for this. I can just hear Tom Brok—"

"Can it, honey," Shatner answered in a deep booming voice. "You weren't on any fact-finding junket this time. Paris Air Show, my ass. You're working for the *Contras*, and you've stolen the hearing aid plans."

"Hearing aid?" Pleia demanded. "What are you talking about?"

"For the Deaf Star," Shatner replied. "Now will you tell us where the plans are, or will we have to get rough?"

"I'll die before I tell you anything!" she cried.

"We'll see about that," Shatner answered, then called over his shoulder: "Bring me the VCR."

A storm trooper wheeled it up. The TV was on—Ted Koppel, looking as cute as ever, asked: "Is the Empire State really a threat? Or is its much-feared fleet just little models?"

Shatner switched to "play." An FBI warning replaced Mr. Koppel, followed by the title for *The Smurfs and the Magic Flute*. Pleia's eyes bugged wide in horror.

"No!" she shrieked, trying to shrink away from the TV. The trooper holding her kept her squarely in front of it, clapping his hands on either side of her head, training her face straight toward the screen. She tried to close her eyes; another trooper pried them open.

"Tell me, Princess," said Darth Shatner.

She kept her resolve till the credits were over. But at the first sight of a little blue body, her will snapped.

"I gave the plans to my robots, Snafu-Detoo and Bee Twennynine," she cried. "Turn it off, in the Script's name, turn it off. . . ."

"First tell me where the robots are," Shatner pressed.

"We sent them ahead in a scout ship when we realized we were going to be attacked."

"A scout ship was picked up by our sensors," one of Shatner's officers confirmed.

"They were bound for Tattooween, Delaware Province," Pleia continued, trembling, sweat pouring from her brow. "I sent them to contact Dobi-Wan Gillis. . . ."

"Dobi-Wan," Shatner mused. "My old mentor—the last of the Knights of Columbus."

"That Catholic group?" asked an Oberlieutenant.

"No, the other one," said Shatner.

"He was my only hope," Pleia gasped, mind going numb in the barrage of inanities emanating from the TV. "Now, turn it off, please."

Shatner ignored her. "Tattooween," he said. "That's in this system, isn't it?"

"The third planet from the double suns," Pleia said. "The one that looks like Hervé

Villechaize."

"Poor planet," Shatner said, shaking his head.

"I told you everything," Pleia moaned. "Now, kill that movie, I beg you."

"Are you kidding?" Shatner asked, pulling up an easy chair, sitting beside her. "This is one of my favorite flicks. Talk about the Dark Side of the Script!" He pointed a black-gloved finger at the TV. "I just love the part coming up here—"

A wail of despair poured from Pleia's throat.

Known as "The Place Where the Universe Meets and Eats," Clemenza's on Rte. 13 in Delaware was Tattooween's busiest bus stop and spaceport, and the intergalactic riffraff quotient was pretty damn high. As Tomokato sat in a wallside booth munching on a well-mustarded soft pretzel and drinking his Diet Dr. Pepper (even though he liked the soft drink very much, he did not quite consider himself a "Pepper"), he gazed dubiously at the weird clientele. Jackboots clicking against the linoleum, a Tyrannosaurus *Gaueleiter* in full Gestapo getup strode arrogantly toward the men's room, having just stepped off a shuttle from the Asteroid of Nazi Dinosaurs; a bad-kneed sailor waiting for the Norfolk bus stood playing an ancient Space Invaders game while several Andalusian Dogs looked on. There were Ganymedean Axolotl-Men, buxom amazons from the Planet of Sexy Women, muscular barbarians from the Planet of Big Strong Men, but strangest of all, Tomokato decided, were those Mummers from South Philly playing a string-band version of the theme from *Patton*; a big Jerry Goldsmith fan, he was more than a little gratified when they caught a wild burst of Kalashnikov fire from some Lebanese having it out in a corner.

He finished his pretzel, wondered briefly how such a snack would go over back in sixteenth-century Japan, then turned his mind once more to the problem of recruiting a space-pilot. He had been told this snack bar was the best place to look, but all the pilots he had talked to so far had balked when they found out what he wanted them for. It was pure madness, they had assured him, trying to hunt down Darth Shatner and Grand Moff Cuomo—especially when it almost certainly meant a trip to the sinister Deaf Star, an armored battle-station capable of wreaking more devastation than Jimmy Carter—put together.

While the cat pondered his situation, he suddenly noticed a familiar face; it was Wisconsin Platt, he was sure of it, even though he was dressed in semiwestern space-rogue duds rather than pulp-adventurer clothes. He was with two other people: an old grey-bearded man and a young blond fellow. The latter had the expression of a cocker spaniel tapped on the head with a sledgehammer, and an Adam's apple roughly the size of a soccer ball. Apparently not seeing the cat in his dimly-lit niche, Platt led them to a table near Tomokato, saying:

"If you're looking for a pilot, I'm your man."

The cat listened hard from then on.

"I'm the guy who made the Wilmington-to-Chester run in forty parsecs," Platt continued. "Maybe you've heard of my ship, the *Century 21*. She's seen a lot of real estate."

"What's your name?" the old man asked.

"Wisconsin Pla—Wisconsin Solo. What's yours?"

"Dobi-Wan Gillis." The old man nodded toward his young companion. "And that's my apprentice, Keye Luke."

"You mean you really know how to drive a spaceship, Mr. Solo?" Keye Luke asked, Adam's apple bobbing up and down like a scenic elevator gone berserk. "What kind of transmission does it have?"

Platt snorted. "Four on the floor. What else, you little twerp."

"Sorry," Keye Luke said, cowering. "I guess you hate me, huh?"

Platt shook his head halfheartedly. "No, it's just that— "

"Oh, go on, hate him," Dobi-Wan broke in. "Everybody else does."

"Look, we're wasting time here," Platt said. "What do you want my services for? And how much are you willing to pay me?"

"More than your wildest dreams," Dobi-Wan replied.

"My wildest dreams aren't about money," Platt answered. "I've got this one where I'm running in slow motion, and . . ."

"As for why we want the ship," Dobi-Wan went on, "it's very simple. We want you to take us to the Deaf Star."

Platt had just been taking his first gulp from

a cup of coffee, but at the mention of the words *Deaf Star*, he sprayed it all over Dobi-Wan in a titanic spit-take worthy of Danny Thomas himself.

"*Deaf Star?*" Platt shouted at the top of his lungs. "Are you nuts? I did some time in there once. Caught me smuggling Coors."

"Isn't it legal to sell Coors in the Empire State now?" Dobi-Wan said, wiping his face off.

"Wasn't then. But anyway, what do you want to go to the Deaf Star for?"

"Because we've come into possession of secret plans that might enable us to sabotage it. For the Rebel Confederation."

At *Rebel Confederation*, Platt let fly another spit-take, but Dobi-Wan ducked this time.

"You're part of the Rebel Confederation?" Platt screamed.

Before Dobi-Wan could answer, two Spies went scurrying from the snack bar.

"Dobi-Wan!" Keye Luke shrieked. "They must be going to tell the garrison!"

"Don't worry," Dobi-Wan answered. "They can't hurt us. You should study the Script more closely."

"Sorry," Keye Luke said.

Dobi-Wan patted him paternally on the shoulder. "You little jerk," he said.

"But how did you get your hands on these plans?" Platt asked.

"Princess Pleia Piano sent them to me with her two robots, Snafu-Detoo and Bee Twenny-nine."

"Robots?"

"Yes. Let me call them over here." Dobi-Wan waved them to the booth, a short dumpy wheeled robot, and a gold-plated humanoid one, both of them rather amusing-looking in a lowest-common-denominator sort of way.

Whipping out a blaster, Platt blew them into pieces of smoking scrap metal.

"Why'd you do that?" Keye Luke demanded.

"Kid," Platt drawled, "I've been from one end of this galaxy to the other, and I've never seen *anything* I hate worse than cute robots."

"Lucky we removed the plans from them," Dobi-Wan said.

"Yeah, I guess so, seeing as how I'm going to take you on this crazy mission."

"You will?" Keye Luke asked excitedly.

"Yeah. I've got some scores to settle with the Empire State. Also, I'm really stupid."

Tomokato picked that moment to break into

the conversation.

"Wisconsin," he called. "Wisconsin Platt!"

But Platt just looked at him, seemingly puzzled.

Tomokato went over to their table. "You don't remember me? The Holy Spad and all that?"

"Come on now, Tomokato," Platt whispered. "I don't want the people around here to know who I am—I've had to adopt a whole new style, lose a couple dozen IQ points . . . Suppose they found out I'm an archeologist? How much smuggling work do you think I'd get if everyone knew I'm an academic type?"

At that, Dobi-Wan spat a mouthful of coffee into *Platt's* face. "An *academic?*" he cried.

Two more Spies left the room.

"I've been listening to your conversation," Tomokato said. "I wonder if you might allow me to join you. On your trip to the Deaf Star, that is."

"Out of the question," Dobi-Wan said.

"Why?" Keye Luke asked. "I like cats."

"The Script never mentioned him," Dobi-Wan answered.

"But the Script doesn't reveal everything.

You've said so yourself."

Dobi-Wan harrumphed. "How do we know we can trust him?"

"Oh, you can trust him," Platt said. "And he might come in handy once we get to the Deaf Star. Very dangerous cat. Fought his way from one end of Spad Castle to the oth—"

A series of shrieks cut him off, and customers scattered. All at once the snack bar was overrun with Imperial SS, the whole mob of them converging on the table, brilliant streaks of white light bursting from their pistols.

Beams flashing all around him, Tomokato started to duck, then realized that no matter what the storm troopers did, they couldn't hit him or his prospective allies at the table for that matter. Drawing both swords, he strode forward; blades whickering, gleaming, he slashed through one arm after another as the troopers tried to grab him. Blood jetting from their truncated limbs, the injured SS retreated, and he gladly gave the same treatment to the ones replacing them—the entire bunch was down to shoulder-stumps before they finally took the hint and dashed from the snack bar.

"Oh come *on,*" came a haranguing voice from outside; their commander's, Tomokato guessed. "What do you *mean* he cut your arms off?"

The cat turned. Platt and Dobi-Wan were still sitting at the table, Keye Luke just poking his head up from under it.

"What did I tell you about this cat?" Platt asked Dobi-Wan, jerking a thumb toward Tomokato.

"I don't know," the old man said. "Perhaps with the proper training . . ."

Flicking the blood from his swords, Tomokato loosed a short, disdainful laugh and sheathed the blades.

"Look, he's coming, and that's all there is to it," Platt said.

"Hadn't we better get out of here?" Keye Luke asked anxiously.

As if to emphasize his point, the SS, thoroughly shamed by their commander, came swarming back into the snack bar, holding their pistols between their teeth, firing with their tongues. Oddly enough, their marksmanship was radically improved. Tomokato and the others raced out a nearby exit amid a hail of laser-bolts.

"Follow me!" Platt cried, leading them through a maze of alien-crowded lanes and alleys, in and out of sewers and subway-tunnels, gas mains, elevator shafts, crawlways, irrigation canals, electrical conduits, and fiber optics; after several hours, the SS gave up and committed suicide long about the middle of the Schuykill Expressway.

Tomokato's group took their time after that, at last entering a picturesquely shabby hangar. In the middle of the floor stood a large plywood boat with torpedo tubes along either side; barely covered with Scotch transparent tape, a jagged crack showed in the side of the hull, as if the whole craft had once been broken in half. On the bow the faint numbers *109* could still be read.

"The *Century 21,*" Wisconsin Platt announced proudly.

"It's a PT boat!" Keye Luke groaned.

"Yeah, but I've made a lot of modifications," Platt answered, flicking the switch to retract the roof doors. "Now if you'll just get aboard . . ."

They went up the ramp, and he opened the cabin. Besides being rendered airtight with loads and loads of duct tape, the interior had been partially upholstered with red plush carpet, floor, walls, and ceiling. A tape deck occupied a central place in the control console, beside a full rack of Abba and Monti Rock III cassettes.

Strapping himself in, Platt fired up the engines. Tomokato wandered toward the back of the cabin and started to sit down on a wooden crate with a strange char mark on the side, in which a Nazi eagle-and-swastika insignia could still be recognized.

"Don't sit on that!" Platt shouted, watching the cat in a rearview mirror. Puzzled, somewhat ruffled by Platt's tone, Tomokato stood.

"Why not?" he asked.

"It's a long story. Take one of these seats up front and buckle yourself down."

Tomokato complied. Moments later, the *Century 21* lifted vertically from the hangar, then accelerated swiftly at a slant. Platt shifted into third, then fourth, leaving the atmosphere far behind.

A red light began to flash on the console.

"What's that?" Keye Luke shouted.

"Scanner's picked up something," Platt replied.

"You mean like that big spaceship up ahead?"

Barely twenty feet from their bow, speeding toward them, was the radio mast of the Empire State Building, a gigantic ape clinging to it with one paw, reaching out for the *Century 21* with the other. Platt brought the PT boat's nose up violently, and they felt the hull shake as the paw just brushed it. Skimming ahead over the surface of the building, too close to the deck for the Imperial Teflon Lasers to be brought to bear, the *Century 21* sped clear of the enemy battleship. But just to make sure, Platt pulled a lever on the console marked Nitrous Oxide. Laughing hysterically, the boat shot forward like a jackrabbit on speed.

"The Empire State Building," Dobi-Wan breathed. "Shatner's ship."

Even as he spoke, they heard it skidding to a stop behind them, obviously preparatory to pulling a one-eighty and coming after them.

"Yeah," Platt said. "And it'll be on our tail all the way to the Deaf Star. They must know we've got the plans."

"Can we maintain our lead?" Tomokato asked.

"Not once they get cracking on all cylinders. . . ." Platt paused. "But there's always the Short Cut."

"Short Cut?"

"Right," Platt replied. "Space warp. It's right up ahead, if only we can reach it in time."

Looking in a side-view mirror, Tomokato saw the Empire State Building gaining rapidly, the giant gorilla taking aim with a titanic Mossberg .306 equipped with a telescopic sight. Two flashes of yellow light erupted from the gun's barrel. The ape was a much better shot than his comrades in the Imperial SS, the slugs grazing the *Century 21*.

"Is there any way to kill that ape?" Tomokato asked.

"Not to kill him," Platt said. "But—" He pressed a button. The port torpedo tube spewed out a white blast of compressed gas, and a long yellow object surged forth—it was a few moments before Tomokato realized it was a massive banana. The ape reached out, grabbed the banana, and peeled it. Smiling blissfully, he took his first bite, thoroughly distracted.

"Works every time," Platt said. "Coming up on the warp now."

Actually, there were two of them, side by side, one marked Deaf Star and Vicinity, the other, Lower Manhattan. Stopping briefly to pay the toll, Platt took the ship into the Deaf Star warp, an instant before the pursuing battle-wagon crashed into the concrete abutment above, slamming the ape straight to concussionville.

"That'll hold 'em up awhile," Platt said. "Knew they wouldn't be able to stop in time."

"But when will they reach the Deaf Star?" Tomokato asked. "I want to meet Shatner—face-to-face."

"You'll get your chance," Dobi-Wan said. "We're going to have a run-in with him—it's in the Script."

"Good," Tomokato said. "Will we meet Cuomo, too?"

"Yes. What do you want with them, anyway?"

"Their deaths. Cuomo ordered Shatner to join the host that murdered My Lord Nobunaga."

"Why?"

"I'm not sure," Tomokato replied. "But I think it had something to do with the fact that My Lord never wore seat belts."

"Bad habit," Dobi-Wan said.

"I know. And he paid for it. But I must avenge him nonetheless."

On and on the boat hurtled through the space warp. Platt eased it to a halt only once, to refill the radiator; then the journey continued.

"We're make really good time," Dobi-Wan said, checking his watch. "The Script be praised."

"You keep mentioning this Script," Tomokato said. "What is it?"

"It's the origin of the universe," Dobi-Wan replied, "the ultimate ground of our being. It creates us and permeates us, knocks us off or lets us live, depending on what would make the best kind of ending."

"And you worship it?"

"Not exactly. 'Try to get in good with it' is a better way of putting it, I think. And speaking of the Script—" Dobi-Wan looked at Keye Luke. "It's about time for another lesson, wouldn't you say?"

"No!" Keye Luke cried, flinching at the mere idea.

"Come on, Luke," Dobi-Wan said. "How do you ever expect to become a Knight of Columbus if you don't have your lessons?"

"Suppose I just bribe you?"

"Ha, ha, ha, ha," Dobi-Wan said with a laugh. "Now get your laser-saber out and put on your helmet, or I'll slap the snot out of you."

Unbuckling himself from his seat, Keye Luke stood, producing the weapon out of his *gi* and switching it on.

"And the helmet," Dobi-Wan said.

Luke pulled it from his pocket and settled it on his head.

"Heads up," Dobi-Wan said, tossing a spherical robot drone at him. Hovering in midair, the drone shot several crimson beams at the old man's apprentice, who managed to deflect them with his saber—just barely.

"Now try it with the blast-shield down," Dobi-Wan said.

"Oh, come on, Dobi-Wan," Keye Luke whined.

"Do it," Dobi-Wan said, in an amicably threatening tone. "Or shall I lock you up with all the E.T. dolls again?"

Immediately Keye Luke snapped the opaque visor down, gulping. Several seconds passed. Then a red bolt shot from the drone. Luke's weapon flashed up to deflect—and missed. His lips were just forming the words *Aww shucks* as the beam struck him full in the chest and splattered him all over the bridge.

Dobi-Wan turned to Tomokato. "Guess the Script wasn't with him," he said cheerfully, flick-

ing a bit of smoking hamburger from his cheek. "Think *you* might like to become a Knight of Columbus?"

"I'll pass," the cat replied.

At length the *Century 21* emerged from the space warp. Dead ahead loomed the Deaf Star.

"Wow," Platt said. "I'd forgotten how big it is."

"See that ear-shaped structure?" Dobi-Wan asked. "The circular object in the middle is the hearing aid, the Deaf Star's main sensor. Neutralize the hearing aid, and the whole station's virtually blind, her exterior fire-control system useless. The only way she could be defended against attack is by fighters launched from inside. Once we take out the hearing aid, we'll notify the Rebel Fleet, which is lurking around here someplace. They'll have a pretty good chance to destroy the primary target."

"Primary target?" Tomokato asked.

"You'll notice that long trench around the station's middle," Dobi-Wan went on. "The primary target's—oh, there it is." The Deaf Star

had been rotating all along, and a blue, white, and red bull's-eye had come into view on a wall at the end of the trench. "Hit that, and the whole station goes. Massive chain reaction—first the petrol dump blows, then the magazine, then the gas mains and the thermonuclear generator."

"All right," Platt said. "But why not just swoop in and attack the hearing aid now?"

"If the fire-control system's still working, we'd never get close enough," Dobi-Wan said. "We have to sabotage it from inside."

"So what's your plan?" Platt asked, guiding the ship closer and closer to the Deaf Star.

"Oh, don't worry," Dobi-Wan said as a swarm of K-winged fighters spewed from a hangar deck directly in front of them. "I'll think of one."

"What?" Platt cried, and turned the ship round. But within moments the hull began to vibrate, and the vessel continued toward the Deaf Star stern first.

"We're caught in a tractor beam!" Platt gritted. "They'll drag us right in!"

"Do you have any place we can hide?"

Tomokato asked.

"Smuggling compartment, below deck. Sensor-proof."

"Let's get inside, quick."

"Right," Platt said. Unstrapping himself, he led them down into the compartment, shutting the lid behind them.

"Got any of that Coors left?" Dobi-Wan asked.

"No," Platt replied. "Just cigarettes and fireworks. There's been a big demand for cherry bombs in the galaxy these days. Don't know why."

"What do you mean?" Dobi-Wan demanded. "Do you know anything better for blowing up toilets?"

After a few minutes the ship stopped vibrating, and they felt it settle to a stop. Presently they heard a hatch sliding back above, and footbeats; the engines were shut off, dieseling a bit before they fell silent.

"Doesn't seem to be anyone on board, sir," a voice said.

"Does this ship look familiar to you?" a second voice asked. "Isn't this the *Century 21*? Wisconsin Platt's vessel?"

"I think you're right, sir. We captured it once, didn't we?"

"And he was hiding in that smuggling compartment. Better check it."

Footsteps thumped close to the compartment hatch.

"Hey!" the underling called. "Hey! Anyone there?"

Shutting his eyes, grimacing with concentration, Dobi-Wan tapped into the Script. "Hell no," he said.

"They said they're not there," the underling relayed.

"Very good. Let's go."

Footsteps receding from the cabin, the sound of the hatch sliding shut.

"Whew," Dobi-Wan said. "Almost blew that one. Caught myself thinking about the Solid Gold Dancers."

They went back up into the cabin. To their shock, they found an SS trooper standing in front of the main hatchway, staring at them.

"Hey, you were down there all along!" he said, raising his pistol.

Drawing his sword, Tomokato bounded forward, slicing, and the plastic-sheathed hand holding the blaster dropped to the floor. As the trooper stopped to pick it up, Tomokato took his head off.

"Couldn't you have taken care of him with your powers?" Platt asked Dobi-Wan.

"Didn't think I should try it," Dobi-Wan replied. "My concentration's definitely off today. What if I started thinking about T and A again?"

"There are worse things to think about," Platt said. "Who's your favorite Solid Gold Dancer, anyway?"

"The lead one, what's her name—the girl with the great legs."

"You mean Darcel? She's not on the show anymore."

"Oh man, really?"

"Really."

"Gentlemen," Tomokato said impatiently, "what do we do now?"

"How's this?" Dobi-Wan asked. "First, we shut the venetian blinds so no one can see in."

They rolled them down.

"And?" Tomokato asked.

"I'm thinking," Dobi-Wan said.

"Okay," Platt said. "How about I put on that dead trooper's getup and march you both toward the detention block? It's right next to the hearing aid's control room. Then if we can stage some sort of diversion . . ."

Tomokato reached down into the smuggling compartment, pulling up a pawful of cherry bombs. "Is there a men's room near the control room?" he asked.

Realizing what he had in mind, Platt grinned, nodding. Dumping the dead SS man out of his plastic armor, he put it on.

"Too bad we can't clean that blood off the front," Tomokato said. Much of the breastplate was splashed with it.

"I'll just tell everyone you gave me a very hard time," Platt said, and opened the hatchway. "Follow me."

"If we're your prisoners, shouldn't you be behind us?" Tomokato said.

"That's such a cliché," Platt replied. "But I guess you're right."

They headed down the ramp.

As Tomokato's party made its way toward the control room, a shuttle from the Empire State

Building landed in the hangar. Darth Shatner and two SS bodyguards emerged, together with Princess Pleia, and went directly to Grand Moff Cuomo's office.

"Governor Cuomo," Pleia said as she laid eyes on him, "I thought I'd find you here. I smelled your foul reek the moment I stepped onto this battlestar."

"I bet you did," Cuomo replied. "I've just got to stop eating chili." He looked to Shatner. "Do you have the plans?"

"Don't *you*?" Shatner asked.

"Why should I?"

"Pleia sent them to Dobi-Wan Gillis, and Dobi-Wan is on the *Century 21*—which is sitting over in the main hangar right now. I transmitted a warning—"

"*What?*" Cuomo demanded, and turned to his secretary, a plump, middle-aged woman with orange hair. "Were there any calls during my lunch break?"

"Something about a captured smuggling vessel," she replied, filing away at her nails. "And one from Mr. Shatner here. But you said you

didn't want to talk to him, so I figured you wouldn't be interested in his messages."

"Didn't want to talk to me, eh?" Shatner asked Cuomo. "Why not?"

"I—I—" Cuomo sputtered.

"It was that article in *People* magazine, wasn't it? The one where they put me on the 'Who's Not Hot' list, right?"

"Right between Suzanne Somers and Boxcar Willie," Cuomo's secretary cackled.

"That's enough out of you," Shatner said, raising a fist, tapping mentally into the Dark Side of the Script. Instantly her throat purpled as if a huge invisible strangling hand had locked onto it; cartilage popped, and her head shot ceilingward at the end of a neck that had been transformed into something very much like a long squirt of toothpaste.

"*People* magazine," Shatner growled. "I find your lack of taste disturbing." His head turreted round toward Cuomo, who was clutching his throat. "You going to take my calls now, or what?"

Cuomo nodded nervously.

"Now, Dobi-Wan's on board this battle-station," Shatner continued. "I saw it in the Script. And he's got the hearing aid plans. We'd better get over to the control center. We can drop the Princess off in the detention block on the way. But first, sound a stage-four alert. The SS can head Dobi-Wan off."

"I don't know how to do it," Cuomo answered. "Madge there"—he nodded toward his secretary's corpse—"used to take care of that sort of stuff for me. All the alarms were routed through her console, too, and she's the only one who knew the user code."

"Ratcrap," Darth Shatner gritted. "Come on."

As Tomokato and his companions drew near the entrance to the control room, they slipped into the men's room on the right side of the hall; but they were barely through the door when an SS Major emerged from a booth and accosted them.

"What are you doing, private?" he asked Platt imperiously.

"Prisoner transfer," Platt replied.

"To the men's room?"

Dobi-Wan raised his hand. "I *reeeally* had to go. . . ."

"And why haven't you disarmed this prisoner?" the Major demanded, indicating Tomokato.

"Big reactor leak, very dangerous," Platt said.

"Huh?" the Major replied, an instant before Tomokato ripped into him with an emergency appendectomy.

"God, what a mess," Platt said, watching the corpse slump to the floor. "We're going to get an R-rating for sure."

Tomokato shook his head resolutely. "PG-13," he answered.

"Better plant those bombs in the hoppers before anyone comes in," Dobi-Wan said.

He stood guard as Tomokato and Platt divided the cherry bombs between them, lit them, and flushed them down the toilets. Then the trio went back out into the corridor, trying hard to look casual, Platt and Dobi-Wan whistling. Unhurriedly, they made toward the control-room door.

The cherry bombs went, one after another. Shouts rang out from the control room and the detention block, crowds of guards rushing from both to see what had happened.

"This is great!" Dobi-Wan said, tickled half to death with the way the plan was working. And then the three of them were in.

The room was empty except for a few technicians glued to their consoles, one of which had a large sign above it reading:

Do Not Insert Chewing Gum in Headphone Jack Here.

"That's what we want," Dobi-Wan said, after hastily consulting the hearing aid plans; thrusting the diagrams back into his robes, he pulled out a piece of Hubba-Bubba and popped it into his venerable old mouth.

The trio crossed to the console.

Its operator looked up, taking off his headset. "What are you doing here?" he asked.

Tomokato ripped the set from the jack; the operator tried to snatch it back from him, but Platt yanked his legendary wet towel from concealment and snapped it out with terrible force, flinging the man back from the console with a red mark on his throat the size of a Mick Jagger hickey. Blood bubbling from his lips, the technician kicked and died.

"Sure hope I got it soft enough," Dobi-Wan

said, pulling the gum from his mouth, jamming it down the jack.

Instantly the console began to sputter and spark. They retreated. The controls burst into flame, then exploded. A huge terminal screen on the wall behind suddenly printed out the words: *HOT DAMN*.

Technicians gawked and shouted, pelted for the door. Dobi-Wan rushed to a transmitter-panel and started in on his message to the Rebel Fleet.

"Dobi-Wan!" boomed a hollow voice. It was Darth Shatner, standing in the doorway, Grand Moff Cuomo on one side of him, Princess Pleia on the other, heavily guarded by SS. Hearing the explosions, Shatner and the troops he had gathered had simply bypassed the detention block.

Dobi-Wan ignored him and continued to transmit his message.

Recognizing Shatner and Cuomo from pictorials in *Empire State Spaceways*, the Luftwaffe-thansa in-flight magazine, Tomokato rushed forward shrieking, *katana* in one paw, *wakazashi*

in the other. Shatner's SS laid down a barrage of laser-beams, but the cat knew enough by now to ignore them completely.

Shatner pulled out his laser-saber and flicked it on, Cuomo leaping behind him. Tomokato never paused, slicing first with his longsword, then with the short; Shatner's saber met both strokes, the white-hot shaft of light ripping through Tomokato's blades in showers of sparks.

Suddenly defenseless, Tomokato jumped back. Shatner charged forward, slashing at his legs. Tomokato leaped over the stroke, only to catch a black-gloved fist under his chin that sent him sailing backward. His head rang, but he kept enough of his wits to drop both hilt-shards and pluck a *shuriken* from his belt; landing flat on his back, he hurled the spiked metal star into the middle of Shatner's black plastic mask. Driving through to the flesh behind, it stuck tight, gleaming above Shatner's breath-grid like a really silly fake nose.

Shatner howled, trying to pull it free; then Dobi-Wan came between him and Tomokato, slashing with his own laser-saber.

Wisconsin Platt, meanwhile, had shucked his helmet and was holding the storm troopers at bay with a rocket-pistol whose shells easily penetrated their armor. Princess Pleia's guards went down in a burst of burning, shattered plastic; she dashed toward Platt, falling madly in love with him the instant she got close enough to really appreciate his roguish good looks, even though she remained loath to admit her true feelings about him to herself, torn as she was between her own fierce independence of spirit and the deep longings for a passionate roll in the hay that were even then stirring inside her late-adolescent bosom.

"Hubba-hubba," he said, gathering her under one arm, leering sidelong at her chubby little face.

She hit him.

Not far away, Tomokato stood watching the battle between Dobi-Wan and Shatner, wondering how to deal with the Dark Lord's laser-saber. He was tremendously impressed by the swordplay on both sides; it seemed almost a shame that he could not simply stand back and

take it all in as a spectator.

Suddenly, as though Dobi-Wan had been reading his thoughts, the old wizard called: "Okay, Tomokato! Get a load of this!"

Raising his sword, he left his midsection wide open.

Shatner paused, apparently amazed that Dobi-Wan would present him with such an opportunity; then he translated him to a higher plane with a slash across the rib cage. Dobi-Wan simply vanished out of his robes, which hung in air for an instant before collapsing.

"Why'd Dobi-Wan let himself be killed?" Tomokato cried to Platt.

"Damned if I know," Platt cried, blasting away joyously at the SS running around behind Shatner.

Shatner nudged Dobi-Wan's robes with his boot. "You old nitwit," he said, "that trick *never* works."

But Dobi-Wan's fallen laser-saber had rolled near the cat; Tomokato snatched it up and rushed at the Dark Lord once more, meeting him blade for blade, driving him steadily back. Platt brought up the rear, shooting any storm trooper who came too close to the battling swordsmen, Pleia making rude comments to him all the while.

There was no sign of Cuomo anywhere.

Past the detention block Tomokato pushed Shatner, back and back along the corridor. Launching stroke after stroke, hammering incessantly on the black-clad giant's defense, he drove him all the way to the hangar; up onto the ramp of the *Century 21* they went, into the cabin. Platt and Pleia scrambled in behind, shut the hatch.

"Help that poor cat!" Pleia cried to Platt.

"He'd be after me next if I took Shatner out," Platt replied, dropping into the control seat, firing up the engines. "Strap yourself in!"

She complied. The ship shot forward through the closed hangar doors, which were, conveniently enough, only styrofoam.

Tomokato and Shatner were hurled back against the rear of the cabin, but quickly resumed their epic battle. Shatner went on the offensive, wounding Tomokato twice, on the arm and across the snout, forcing the cat into a corner. The Dark Lord laid on a storm of blows, almost bashed the sword from Tomokato's paws. But Tomokato managed to parry each stroke, and finally Shatner stepped back, breathing heav-

ily, asthmatically.

"Give up, cat," he said.

"Never," Tomokato panted.

"Your heart's not in it," Shatner went on. "I can sense the confusion in you. You don't want to kill me."

"What are you talking about?" Tomokato demanded. "You helped murder My Lord."

"You don't understand what's happening. The Script runs strong in you, even if you don't realize it. And you sense the truth about us. That's what's weakening you."

"What truth?"

Shatner spoke slowly, measuring the words: "That I . . . am your father."

Keeping his sword in ready position, Tomokato squinted at him, pondering this.

"But how can that be?" he asked at last. "When I'm your father?"

Shatner lowered his sword. "Really?"

Tomokato stepped forward and sliced him through with a single devastating diagonal stroke.

"Daddy!" Shatner cried, an awful note of pain and accusation in his voice, the top half of his body sliding slowly downward, an enormous gust of blood erupting from his heart and lungs, spraying the ceiling.

"I think you might be right, Wisconsin," Tomokato cried as the black-robed body crumpled before him.

"About what?" Platt asked.

"That R-rating," Tomokato said, switching off the laser-saber.

"Glad you're cat enough to admit it," Platt said, taking the ship farther and farther from the Deaf Star, passing the oncoming Rebel Fleet in the process.

"And now for Cuomo," Tomokato said.

"What?" Platt demanded. "We're not going back there!"

"But we have to!" Pleia cried. "Our fleet's going to need all the help it can get."

"Hey, I might be stupid, but I'm not that stupid," Platt answered.

She batted her eyelashes at him. "Oh, yes you are. Even dumber, maybe."

"That's true," he admitted.

"I love you," she said.

Swerving the ship round, he took it into the

thick of the battle that had joined between the Rebel Fleet and K-winged fighters from inside the Deaf Star; swarming to protect the Primary Target, the Imperial craft turned back every attack. Platt blasted several K-Wings with his lasers and even made a pass at the target, firing his remaining banana; but the Empire State Building had come into the fight by then, and the ape on the radio-mast, head bandaged, snatched the fruit before it could strike home.

"This would be a lot more exciting if there was some music or something," Pleia observed, watching the battle.

"Got just the thing." Platt reached into his tape-rack for an old John Williams cassette; with the theme from *Lost in Space* blaring through his loudspeakers, he destroyed several more Imperial fighters.

But his rebel allies were not doing so well. Outnumbered and outgunned, the survivors were soon in full retreat.

"Time to git," Platt said.

"No!" Pleia cried.

"Hell, I don't even have anything heavy enough to destroy the target anymore."

"Do you have a spacesuit?" Tomokato asked.

"Yeah, why?"

"Just let me put it on—then skim the surface of the Deaf Star."

"What do you have in mind?"

"You'll see. Just do as I say."

Platt steered the ship away from the Deaf Star, pursued by a whole flock of K-Wings; suddenly he hit the brake, bringing the ship to a rubber-burning halt, and the enemy craft screamed past. Stabbing his fingers into the laser-controls again and again, he sent burst after burst into their glowing exhausts, blowing the K-Wings to burning smithereens.

"Got that suit on yet?" he cried.

Tomokato settled the helmet down over his own and switched on the communicator. "Yes. Take us back in. And remember, get me as close to the battle-station as you can."

Turning his receiver to the Deaf Star frequency, he heard Cuomo identifying himself by name, giving orders to the Empire State Building and the remaining K-Wings.

Still aboard, the cat thought. *Good. He won't have time to escape.*

But as he entered the airlock and depressurized it, he heard another voice, Dobi-Wan's,

speaking inside his mind:

Read the Script, cat, the old wizard's disembodied spirit said. *Read the Script.*

To Tomokato's amazement, a ghostly loose-leaf folder materialized before him; he took it, and it fell open to page ninety-two. Instantly his eyes were drawn to a sentence midway down— "But at the last moment, Tomokato hesitates, and dies horribly in a hail of fire from the K-Wings."

Told you you should've become a Knight of Columbus, Dobi-Wan chuckled.

Tomokato swore, dropping the Script. Then, as the outer hatch opened, he strode out onto the hull, molecular sticky-shoes gripping the plywood surface. Switching the laser-saber back on, he assumed a ready position on the edge of the deck.

You're going to die, he thought. *You're going to hesitate and die in agony, and all for nothing.*

The Empire State Building careened close; the tail end of the banana still protruding from his mouth, the ape readied his .306, drawing a bead on the cat. He snapped off a shot, missed; the *Century 21* rocketed past him, and Tomokato

drove a devastating kick into the banana's tip, knocking it back into the ape's throat. Looking over his shoulder, the cat saw the ape coughing, choking, trying to reach a finger down his windpipe. Tomokato paid him no further heed.

But what does it matter? he thought. *You can't win.*

He looked toward the Deaf Star. Soon it filled his whole field of vision, a titanic expanse of white, the ear rising from the surface like a giant fungus-growth, the hearing aid sparking and spewing out vapor.

"Closer, closer," he said to Platt, speaking into his transmitter. "As close as you can."

Hardly had he finished when the laser-beams started raining down around him, and the *Century 21* was enveloped in a whirling storm of enemy ships.

Inside the cabin, Platt drained his laser power-cells bone-dry and switched over to his auxiliary systems, the remote-controlled quad fifty machine guns mounted fore and aft. Shredded to pieces, K-Wings tumbled past, pilots bailing out, parachute silk streaming behind them. He nailed a Stuka shooting in on the port side, blew up a Mig 25 just as it was about to crash into the bow; an ornithopter manned by Leonardo da Vinci himself exploded in flames. Pterodactyls retreated with beakfuls of steel-jacketed slugs. Running the gauntlet of Imperial craft, Platt brought the *Century 21* up alongside the Deaf Star.

"Full throttle!" Tomokato cried over the intercom.

Platt floored the pedal, and the ship accelerated violently. In the rearview he saw Tomokato slash once with the laser-saber as the battle-station blurred past. Then the Deaf Star was shrinking swiftly astern.

What good did that do? Platt wondered to himself.

Moments later, Tomokato reentered the cabin and took his helmet off.

"Now listen, cat!" Platt said. "We're getting the hell out of here, and that's all there is to it!"

"Very well," Tomokato said, sounding surprisingly resigned, settling into the seat beside Pleia's and strapping himself in.

"What exactly did you try to do?" Platt demanded.

"Try?" Tomokato asked.

"Look!" Pleia shouted, pointing to the side-view mirror. Platt's jaw sagged as he looked. A neat black slice bisected the Deaf Star, already beginning to fill with blood. The top half of the battle-station lifted slowly from the bottom; then came the awesome orange flare of a thermonuclear blast as the Deaf Star's main power plant went.

Platt swiveled round, gaping at Tomokato. The cat looked at him impassively, blowing on the claws of his left paw.

Some time later, the *Century 21* landed back on Tattooween in a vacant lot not far from Clemenza's. Tomokato went down the ramp, halted at the bottom, turned, and looked back at Platt and Pleia; Platt had his arm around the Princess's waist, and both of them seemed pretty pleased with the situation.

"You sure you won't come back with us to Rebel Headquarters?" Pleia called. "We'll decorate you. Top honors. We've got these little gold stars we glue on your forehead, and—"

"It wouldn't be proper," Tomokato said. "I

did what I did not to help your cause, but to secure vengeance for my Master."

"Oh well," Pleia said.

"We'll miss you at the ceremony," Platt said. "I hope you don't mind if they give me your stars."

"Certainly not," Tomokato replied.

"Where you off to now?"

"Earth. I'm going to take the Metroliner."

"The real world, eh?"

"Of course. That's where all the *worst* villains are. Farewell, both of you." Turning on his heel, the cat strode off toward Clemenza's. But before he got too far from the *Century 21*, he heard a loud slap behind him.

"You've got more hands than an octopus!" Pleia cried.

"You love it honey, admit it," answered Wisconsin Platt.

She giggled.